The
Baggy-Kneed Camel
Blues

Daniel McVay

Knights
Press

Stamford, Connecticut

Designed by Able Reproductions, copyright 1984

Published by Knights Press, P.O. Box 454, Pound Ridge, NY   10576

Library of Congress Cataloging in Publication Data

McVay, Daniel.
  The baggy-kneed camel blues.

  I. Title.
PS3563.C9B3   1984   813'.54   84–14326
ISBN 0–915175–03–7

Printed in the United States of America

To
JOHN and REKO

1. Gesundheit!

"Gesundheit!" she said.

"I beg your pardon," I replied. We were standing on a pier in Barcelona on a hot summer afternoon, waving to people on a luxury liner. I didn't know anyone on the ship. I didn't know her either, for that matter.

"Oh good, you speak English," she said.

"But why did you. . . ?" I tried to get in, unsuccessfully.

"I'm Canadian," she went on. "You must be American."

"It shows?"

"It shows."

It showed because I'm average. Everything. I am average in height, weight, build, looks and hair. And, being a middle-class young man from California, I have no accent at all — no distinction in my voice — just plain old flat, bland Americanese.

She, on the other hand, could have been from just about any place. She was petite, had red hair, green eyes and a few freckles in amongst her tan. She spoke with an international accent. It was a little voice, but it carried well. She may have been a leprechaun.

"Anyway, I didn't sneeze," I said, trying to get back on the subject.

"I know," the leprechaun replied.

Talking to her was like pulling teeth. "So why, then, did you say 'Gesundheit!' to me?"

"I didn't say it to you. I said it to me." She had a lingering giggle in her voice. It wasn't a mocking giggle — just a happy one.

"But you didn't sneeze either," I said.

"I know. Think about it," she said. "Why do we say 'Gesundheit!' or 'bless you' when someone sneezes?"

"Something about the heart skipping a beat?" I was not sure I was keeping up my end of this conversation. I just knew I wanted to be a part of it.

"Exactly . . . sort of," she continued. "So when I saw that man up there on the ship, my heart skipped at least three beats and I said 'Gesundheit!' to myself."

"What man?" I had to know immediately.

"That man," she pointed.

"Gesundheit!" I said, forgetting to close my mouth.

"Oh," is all she said.

I'm usually only attracted to people who have some little oddity about them . . . an imperfection . . . some kind of distinction like one eye being just a little off. Or an odd nose. Left-handed is good. One dimple instead of two has a nice look to it. Accents. Imagine going through life looking for a cross-eyed, left-handed Australian with a broken nose.

That's why I was surprised by the mild tremor that ran through my body when I looked up at the young Apollo, or his Norse equivalent, standing above us on that ship. Tall and tan, blond and beautiful was the short of it. He was your basic Viking hunk, if I may be redundant. I admit I was blinded by his beauty. For all I could see at that moment, he could have had webbed hands and feet. Hey, wouldn't that be kinky? (Weeks later I happily discovered that one of his ears was lower than the other.)

Perfection scares the hell out of me, which may have had something to do with why my knees were shaking as we stood there waving at him.

"Do you know him?" I asked.

"No. Do you?"

"No," I said.

One of the games I play with myself is guessing people's names before I meet them. I had already surmised that my newfound friend's name was one of the Patricialike names, such as Patsy or Patty or possibly Tricia. Trish! She told me earlier that she was Canadian, so I put her in Montreal because they speak English and French there. Then I gave her Irish parents and a college education with a major in drama and a minor in early childhood education. I also guessed she was on vacation with a maiden aunt who was at this very moment terrorizing some poor shopkeeper, looking for a lace shawl to take home to her seventy-three-year-old also-maiden sister with whom she shares a cottage on the outskirts of Toronto. (Score ten points for each correct guess. As you'll discover later, my score for the day was zero.)

As for the young man on the ship, I was praying that he wasn't an Olaf. I could never bring myself to call him Oly. (Olie? Oley? How the hell do you spell Ole?) I decided he should be Erik (with a *k* because it's stronger than *c*) and that he was Norse—a direct descendant of the god Thor. That's as far as I got.

"Keep waving," the possible Trish standing next to me said.

"I come down here about once a week and wave," I said, waving. "I get a strange feeling waving good-bye to people I've never met and never will meet because they're off to some exotic port of call. I fantasize about going with them, knowing I'll probably never get on a luxury liner, much less leave the harbor."

I'm not sure why I have this obsession with tearful good-byes. Sometimes I think it must have something to do with my ever-present need to escape. Whatever I get myself into, I'm always wanting to get out of it. And usually cannot. So I go to docks and airports and train and bus stations to say good-bye—all the time wishing it was me leaving instead of them.

Then again, I sometimes wonder if it isn't all caused by the movies. Like me, movies are always running to docks and to airports and to bus and train stations to have tearful good-byes. Remember Fonda and Redford at the end of *The Electric Horseman*? And there was Hepburn and that Italian singer in *Summertime*. Richard Gere and Lisa Whatsername in *Yanks*. And who could ever forget Tallulah waving from her dinghy in that old classic *Lifeboat*? There are hundreds of them. And they always play up the sounds. The train whistle is an anxious cry of regret. The whoosh of the bus door is like the sealing of a bank vault—so final! And that huge, deep moan of the ship's horn always sounds like it's lost in a fog or is about to hit an iceberg, which is exactly the way your heart feels when they throw those sounds at you.

"I prefer greeting the arriving ships," Trish the leprechaun said. "It's more adventurous. There's always a chance of meeting someone exciting, of starting out on a new relationship."

"I'd rather see them off," I interrupted.

"That's because it's safer," she interrupted my interruption.

"No way," I protested, then asked, "What do you mean, safer?"

"Safer. As in afraid of meeting new people . . ."

She was right in a way. I don't handle those first encounters well at all. "I remember this one really hot night a few years ago," I interrupted again, "I was out for a late walk, trying to cool off, and I passed this guy on the sidewalk. We exchanged some sort of polite greeting and went our separate ways."

"Safer," she gloated.

"I turned back to look at him about half a block farther down the street," I said, trying to ignore her gloating, "and saw that he was also looking back. I slowly wandered off onto this dark side street and then into a small, even darker patio at the rear of an office building and . . ."

"How was he supposed to see you?"

"Do you have to comment?"

"Yes."

"*A few seconds later*, the guy walked around the corner at the other end of the building and stood there silently. I was standing in the shadows, out of the moonlight, and figured he couldn't see me, so I quickly put a cigarette in my mouth and fumbled for my lighter. Then I remembered that I couldn't find the damn thing when I left the apartment and had grabbed an old book of matches. I dug them out of my pants pocket and tried to light one. It wouldn't. I tried another. Nothing. They must have been soggy or just too old. I went through the whole book of matches and never got even a spark. When I finally looked up toward the guy, he was gone. I didn't try to find him."

"See? Afraid of relationships, afraid of any kind of commitment, afraid of . . ." She was still harping on that!

"It isn't that at all!" I argued. "I don't feel anything when they're coming in. On the other hand, I do feel something when they're going out."

"I hate seeing ships off," she said. "It's so sad. It's like saying good-bye to loved ones you'll never see again. It's just too depressing."

"Then what are you doing here now?" I asked.

"Well, I don't know about you, but I'm here waving a big hello to a large number of strangers who are at this very moment arriving in Barcelona on this beautiful ship," she replied. She had a way of sounding pleasant and sarcastic at the same time. I don't know how she did that.

"Good-bye," I corrected.

"Hello!" she insisted.

"No," I wavered.

"What you have to do is stand perfectly still and stare at the side of the ship in relation to the edge of the dock. When they're moving this slowly, it's hard to tell which way they're going," she instructed. This time it was more of the pleasant and less of the sarcastic.

I did.

"Now do you see?" It's definitely on the way in," she said.

"Oh," is all I said. Talk about embarrassing! There I was waving my arm off at these people, all the time thinking they were leaving, and the goddamn boat was on the way in!

"You are afraid," she said. That time she made her voice sound like she was genuinely concerned about me, but was goading me at the same time. I don't know how she did that either, but I responded to the goad rather than to the concern.

"What the hell do you know about it? What the hell do you know about me?" I argued rationally. Okay, so it was emotionally. You'd be emotional too if a total stranger was picking on you about your fears, even if you did like her from the minute she first spoke to you and she was a lovable, red-haired, green-eyed pixie. So what if I'm a little apprehensive about a few things? It's not as though I hide from people. I don't have agoraphobia, for chrissakes! Who did she think she was? Did she think she knew me better than I knew myself?

"Who do you think you are?" I blurted out. "Do you think you know me better than I know myself? Who is that man taking his arm?"

"Who? Where?"

"There!"

An older man had just taken our Viking by the arm and they were walking along the rail toward the gangplank. The man reeked of money. He was about fifty and dressed very expensively. He was round. And woolly. He had reddish-brown hair with little tufts of white around the ears. He looked a lot like a Teddy Bear.

I used to fuck my Teddy Bear. His name was Sam. Between the ages of seven and approximately eleven, before I discovered the boy next door, I stuck my peepee into just about everything I could find in my room that was stickable. Teddy Bear Sam was my favorite. Besides the armpits and crotch, he had a big, soft mouth which opened wide and I'd stick it in there and clamp the mouth closed with my hand and just go to town on the little whore. It was fine until I started ejaculating. He got to be such a mess that I had to cremate him . . . in the incinerator. I cried. Imagine having to burn your first lover! The Mother caught us once. It was early in the affair (pre-ejaculatory, so he was still clean), and I was supposed to be having my after school nap. I had missed Teddy Bear Sam something awful that day (the Bitch wouldn't let me take him to school), so we were getting it on. I was banging away at his left armpit, and I guess I must have gotten carried away in my passion, because I had ridden the little sucker up against the wall. We were knocking the Raggedy Ann and Andy pictures right off their hooks and they were smashing to the floor behind the bed. That's when the Mother came running in, wide-eyed and screaming obscenities. It took me a few seconds to gather my wits about me and to come up with the story that Teddy Bear Sam and I were primitive tribesmen (hence our nakedness) and that, as part of some tribal ritual, our chief had ordered us to fight to the death. She believed it. What choice did she have? The alternative was just too incredible for her to consider.

"Look, he's with his father," the leprechaun said.

"I think the word you're looking for is Daddy, as in Sugar," I corrected.

"Do they still call them that?" she asked.

"I don't know." I didn't.

"Well, whatever they call them these days, he is not one of them. And I'm willing to bet on it."

We bet dinner on it.

As we watched Viking and his Daddy making their way along the deck, I was wondering what the hell I was doing, standing on a Barcelona pier with a woman-girl I didn't know, arguing with her about whether or not I was afraid to meet people, waving to a Viking on an incoming ship which I had thought was an outgoing ship, and betting a dinner, which I couldn't afford to buy anyway, on said Viking's morals and sexual preferences.

"Let's get closer," she suggested, dragging me by the arm behind her. For a petite, she was strong.

We pushed our way in amongst the waiting loved ones and braced ourselves for the onslaught of deboarding passengers. They were just coming down the gangway as we arrived. Viking hesitated right in front of me, looked into my eyes and smiled. His teeth were white-white and his eyes were blue-blue. I froze.

Have you ever felt beige? Standing next to me was a cute, fairy-like woman with red hair and green eyes and just the right amount of freckles, wearing a bright green blouse and pastel green shorts. Standing in front of me was a tall, young man with golden hair, bronze skin and twinkling teeth, wearing a powder-blue shirt and sun-bleached trousers. Then, there was me. Beige hair, beige eyes, beige skin . . . and I was undoubtedly wearing beige clothes or something very close to it. My wardrobe is that way. I started to say that at least it was better than gray, but gray is the other look I have . . . when I'm not being beige.

"Come along, Günter," the older man said to the younger man, in a decidedly British accent.

Günter! The name alone causes chemical changes! My Viking must be a German. The Vikings were Germans—not in the national sense as in Germany, but as in "groups of people in Europe of related language and culture . . . who gave rise to the present cultures of *Scandinavia*, Germany, Austria. . . ." This is according to the *Columbia-VIKING Desk Encyclopedia*.

Günter! My imagination exploded. I could see the two of us to-gether at one of Mad King Ludwig's Bavarian castles. Günter was a count. I don't know what of. I was a captain in the army. Ludwig was off in Paris having dinner with Louis and Marie and we were being attacked by the Russians or the Prussians or whoever was attacking the Germans in those days. We tried to hold them off from a hill in front of the castle, but they were pushing us back farther and farther until our backs were literally up against the castle wall. Count Günter was shouting orders left and right. Soldiers were dying all around us. The roar of the cannons was deafening. The enemy just kept closing in on us! I turned to Günter for instructions. He wasn't there! I or-dered my men to stand and fight to the last man. I took a newly loaded rifle from the little red-haired boy in the green shirt who was behind me. I raised it to my shoulder, aimed, and fired at the man who was charging right at me. He fell. I took another loaded rifle from the boy, but before I could aim, the wounded soldier in front of me raised his rifle with his last ounce of strength and fired! At me! The bullet entered my left shoulder near the heart. I felt nothing at first, just the wetness of my shirt sticking to my chest, but then I felt an extraor-dinary burning sensation and I passed out. When I came to, the boy was trying to give me water. I turned my head and saw Günter! He had returned! He took off his battle-torn shirt and ripped it into strips to bandage my shoulder. He lifted my head gently onto his knee, took the ladle from the boy and gave me a drink of water. He raised his hand, bloodied from my wound, and brushed the hair away from my eyes. I fainted. It may have been from the incredible pain that was surging through my body, but sometimes I wonder if it might not have been from his touch. (Daydreams sure get squishy sometimes, don't they?)

Günter! I could see me standing on a pier with a red-haired pixie in green, waving to him as he walked out of my life forever with his father, or whatever.

Actually, that is exactly what I was seeing.

Günter and his dad were greeted by a chauffeur who led them off to a white limousine.

She hit me on the back, screaming, "Breathe!"

I did. It made me dizzy.

"See? That wasn't so bad," she said.

"Not bad? The blood all left my head. My automatic nervous system switched to manual and I wasn't there to take over! Not bad?!" I ranted.

"Get ahold of yourself, man," she scolded.

"He was staring at me," I said.

"Oh come on. He glanced at you and smiled."

"Glanced at me and smiled?! What he did was stop right there in front of me, turn to me, stare straight into my soul with those incredible blue eyes . . . and then smiled," I insisted.

"God, he barely hesitated," she said. She must've been really jealous to have been going on like that.

"I was there! I saw what he did!"

"I was there too!" she shouted.

"What could you see from down there?" I blurted, regretting it immediately.

People shouldn't make short jokes, especially in anger. They're cruel. I wouldn't have done it if she hadn't been trying so hard to destroy my illusions. Really. Short jokes ("Well at least it saves wear and tear on your knees."), tall jokes ("While you're up, would you hand me one of those coconuts?") and fat jokes ("Hey, like your new shirt. Omars?") are degrading to both the joker and the jokee. Funny thing about human nature, though, is that the worst offenders are often those with the condition. That is self-degrading, but it does seem less offensive that way. It's like complaining about someone in your own family or making derisive jokes about them. It's all right for me to make nasty jokes about the Mother, but I don't like it if my friends do. But then I don't like it if my friends say anything nice about her either. The truth be known, I insist that my friends ignore the Mother altogether.

Fortunately, my young, untall, woman friend chose to ignore my rude reference to her height. "You should've said something to him."

"Like what?" I wondered.

"Oh, hello is a good word for such occasions." There was that sarcasm again.

"What if he doesn't speak English?" I snapped back.

"The man spoke to him in English, dummy! Besides, everyone knows what hello means. It's like love. They're universals." She was getting mean.

"Please. You're wearing me out." She really was.

"It's like tarantula shit," she said.

"Huh?"

"Tarantula shit . . . on bananas," she explained. "You know, the brown, gunky stuff you find up by where they're all hooked together. It's repulsive as hell when you first see it, but when you stop to think about it, you realize that it's going to be thrown out with the peel anyway. Then you don't care anymore! See?" She was nuts.

"Oh . . . sure," I said.

"You don't understand," she said impatiently.

"I'm afraid not." Truthfully, I was afraid to understand.

"Don't you see?" she went on. "You can't worry about all that little preliminary stuff. What is important is getting down to the banana!"

"I'll try to remember that," I was barely able to get out before the laughter hit and the tears began.

"See that you do. Now, let's go to dinner. I seem to owe you one. No way was that guy his father."

"But it's only three o'clock in the afternoon," I protested between the giggles.

"We'll have cocktails first then," she said and then announced, "I'm Stacey," as though it were a magic word.

I think it was.

"Tad," I said, "and you can't imagine how happy I am to meet you!"

I really meant that. My great plan for personal freedom just didn't seem to be working. I'd had all these grandiose ideas about how if I wasn't being smothered by school or work or family and friends that my mind would blossom with creativity and enlightenment . . . and love! It blossomed all right—into seclusion and loneliness.

I knew the minute I saw her that Stacey would bring me out of my withdrawal. Yeah! Magic! Now I won't have to throw myself under the ship's propellers!

First we shook hands. Then we hugged. Then we kissed. Then we hugged again.

2. A Burnous Is A Kaftan Is A Robe

"So Tad, you're gay, huh?" Stacey said.

Jesus H. Christ! (Harold?) What kind of society do we live in that one man can't admire another man's good looks without everyone jumping to the conclusion that he's homosexual? Women compliment each other's appearance all the time and people don't start yelling "Dike!" all over the place. Beauty is beauty, after all. If a man is handsome and/or sexy, I think other men should be able to say so without fear of being labeled by society.

"Yes," I said.

"What's it like?" she asked.

"Haven't you been to bed with a man?"

"Of course."

"Well then you know."

"Oh, yeah, I guess I do," she said, putting still another piece of bread into her soup (*pan en sopa*), then into her mouth (*pan y sopa en boca*). "You do that?!!"

I had the feeling she was imagining something more exotic than the stereotypical picture of some man's *picha* in my *boca*. I say this because of her violent physical reaction—that of spitting an entire slice of *sopa*-soaked *pan* out of her *boca*, across the table and into my lap, thus creating what was possibly the world's first *sopa*-soaked *picha*—mine!

Suddenly, the gypsy was in my lap!

But, I haven't told you about him yet and he does require explanation. After about three-too-many cocktails, Stacey and I ambled up *Las Ramblas* (Barcelona's beflowered, bebookstalled, bemusicianed, bemimed main drag) in search of food, disagreeing in front of every *café y restaurante* as to what it was we wanted to eat.

"I can't eat Chinese food in Spain."

"You would eat sushi in a country that leaves its milk sitting out in eighty-five degree heat?"

"Tacos are not Spanish; they are Mexican."

That's when I saw the waiter—a gypsy if I ever saw one! Black hair. Black eyes. Not a hell of a lot bigger than the leprechaun I was with, but cute as a Teddy Bear, if you know what I mean. I demanded that we go into that café, telling Stacey some lie about how I'd been there before and how good the food was. She wanted to know why it was, if the food was so damned good, that I couldn't remember what kind of food they served. I dragged her inside.

The hostess greeted us, then turned us over to the maître d' (this was not a posh place by any means—they just believe in employment over there), who obligingly seated us near the front windows where I'd noticed the gypsy was working.

I put on my glasses (beige-rimmed of course). A busboy brought water. I took off my glasses. Someone brought menus. I put on my glasses. We studied our menus. I lit a cigarette. Stacey lit a cigarette. Or rather, she put one in her mouth and sat there with it dangling from her lips until I got around to lighting it. I took off my glasses.

"Why are you doing that?" she asked between the cute little puffs she was making on her cigarette—a cigarette, I might add, that was as long as her petite hand.

"Doing what?"

"The glasses. On. Off. On. Off."

"Oh. Don't you know about glasses? See, some people are attracted to people who wear glasses and other people are completely turned off by them. So, if you wear glasses, you've got to split up the times you're wearing them and when you're not. Otherwise, you cut your field in half—your field of possible liaisons, that is. The problem is that, if you do strike up with someone, you don't know whether it was the glasses-look or the nonglasses-look that attracted them in the first place. So, you aren't sure . . ."

"Please! I got it," she interrupted.

I was only trying to explain.

The gypsy was standing at my side. I reached for my glasses, but Stacey grabbed them before I could get to them.

I swear my face was only six inches from his crotch. I wanted to bite it. I didn't.

"*Thenor, ¿que quiereth a comer?*"

Good god! I didn't think they *th*poke Ca*th*tillian here. My high school Spanish isn't up to this. What the hell, give it a try.

"*Yo no thé, pero thi uthted . . .*"

"I*th* not ni*th*e to mock people," gyp*th*y li*th*ped.

I blushed. "Don't do that."

"What?"

"Change languages like that! It short-circuits my brain. and I wa*th*n't, WASN'T mocking you. I was trying to speak Castillian."

"Oh, we don't *th*peak Ca*th*tillian here."

Stacey giggled. I was embarrassed. I was shattered. I was face-to-crotch with a stereotype! No matter what gays do to straighten up their image, the flamboyants will always be there. And, in my experience, there is nothing nellier than a Spanish queen. Apologies to Isabella.

We ordered in English, trying to remain straight-faced amid multiple kicks under the table.

"Do you think he's gay?" Stacey asked after the gypsy minced off to the kitchen.

"Boy, do we have to talk."

Now, back to my *sopa*-soaked *picha* and the gypsy in my lap. Or rather the gypsy hands in my lap, pretending to mop up *sopa* while spending an inordinate amount of time on and around my *picha*, now enlarged. I politely removed his hands, blushed and gave Stacey a dirty look in response to her rude giggling.

The gypsy danced away.

"Kind of cute, huh?" she snickered.

"I suppose," I lied.

"Oh come on! You wore the bridge off your nose trying to get him to notice you."

I absentmindedly reached for my glasses. She must have put them in her purse.

"May I have my glasses back please?"

"Don't pout. Confess, you find him attractive, don't you?"

"I did . . . until he opened his mouth."

"Isn't that a bit snobbish?"

"No."

I don't know, I thought. Maybe a little. How do you tell the difference between snobbery and legitimate likes and dislikes? Why is she picking on me again?

"One of the gays in our group is effeminate and I think he's nice," she said.

"What's our group?"

"Magazine sales. There's five of us. Six, if you count the lech. We run around all over southern Europe trying to get businesses to subscribe to the new *Reporte Internationale* that will revolutionize world markets. Baloney!"

"Sounds like fun," I guessed.

"Sometimes."

"Didn't you say you were from Canada? How'd you get involved in European magazine sales?"

"In a word, Dierdre."

"Dierdre?"

"Dieeerdre . . . and her beau Biffff. My best friend from college and her fiAHNce. Drips both."

"Your best friend is a drip?"

"She is now. Wasn't then. Or didn't seem so much like one then. Met Biff. Dripped. Anyway, she talked me into it—a summer lark—so, there's me, Dierdre, Biff, the lech and Mike and Toby, our other loving couple. Some group."

"Who's the lech?"

"He is supposed to be our supervisor, the group leader. Company man and all that. Instead of supervising, he spend all his time slobbering on women. He's disgusting."

"What's a little slobber among friends?"

"He masturbates in his room at night," she added.

"Are you deliberately trying to embarrass me?"

"Don't you masturbate?" she asked too loudly.

"Of course. Will you please keep your voice down? People are listening." They weren't. Most of the people there probably didn't speak English, except our waiter and he would have loved this conversation.

"No one is listening," Stacey said. "Don't tell me a little frank conversation embarrasses you? You didn't seem to mind it so much when the waiter was feeling you up."

Good god! The woman's a maniac! I fumbled with the check. The gypsy, who apparently was eavesdropping on our conversation, fled in tears. Stacey laughed.

We gathered our things together, paid and went back out on the street.

The night air was refreshing, but once my blush went away, I started to get cold. We huddled against each other on a bench on *Las Ramblas* to keep warm.

Stacey started asking me questions about my experiences with women. I got the distinct impression that she was thinking about converting me back to the opposite sex.

People worry about gays trying to convert straights, but let me tell you, there are a hell of a lot more heterosexuals out there trying to straighten out homosexuals than the other way around. Men and women.

At least she couldn't use the old ploy about how would I know I didn't want to be with a woman if I hadn't tried it. After my best friend and frequent bedmate moved away at the beginning of high school, I dated a lot of girls and even went all the way with one after the Prom in the downstairs kitchen of the Elks Lodge. Her father was an Elk. And in college, I lived with a woman until my best friend at that time, and maybe still now, came along and they fell in love. Oh well. So anyway, I had tried it. And I did like it. I may again sometime. Who knows? But, what I did not like, do not like is anyone trying to cure me. There is nothing to cure. Besides, at that place and time, what I wanted was more experience on the gay side of things.

Stacey said she understood about Toby not wanting to go back to

women because he was effeminate, which is when I interrupted with
a tirade about clichés and myths and ignorance and . . . and then I
shut up because I had started to shout at her and the very last thing
I wanted or needed at that moment was to fight with my newfound
friend.

I asked her to forgive me for my outburst and suggested that we
go have another drink someplace. She did. We did.

We went to a bar around the corner and up a couple of blocks.
El Molino Rojo. The Red Mill. A noisy place. Noisy enough to cover
our conversation in case she insisted on being frank, as she called it.
I ushered us to a booth near the back in a corner.

"Trish?! Trish? You would have me be a Trish?" she was ranting.

I had just told her about the little game I had played on the pier,
guessing her name.

"It's not such a bad name," I said.

"Not bad? It's awful. It's like Dierdre. Cold. Snobbish. Moosh. Trish.
Squoosh!"

"Really Trish," I dared.

"Tadpole!"

"Uh!" I turned white.

"Aha! Rang a bell did I? Let me guess. It was in high school. Senior
year. You were still playing with girls in those days and she was, uh,
cute and, uh, squooshy. Aha! She was a Trish! And you were her little
Tadpole?"

I would have to learn not to attack this woman. I always got the
worst of it.

"She was a Babs," I confessed. "And very squooshy."

We both laughed. Our drinks arrived.

"A toast!" Stacey offered. "To Tadpole and Trish! May they burn in hell!"
Chugalug.

"How do you know he masturbates in his room every night!" I asked.

"Who?"

"There's more than one?"

"Oh, him. Because he books our rooms and makes sure that he gets the one next to ours and because he's a fat slob and because he groans a lot in there and because he rubs up against the wall, moaning, 'Oh Dierdre. Oh Stacey.' Yech!"

I had this vision of a huge, hairy slug, standing in a motel room leering at the wallpaper, flogging away at his whanger or whanging away at his flogger while fantasizing about the two women on the other side of the wall. Suddenly, he falls to his knees and begins to lick the wallpaper furiously, rubbing his sagging, hairy teats against the wall. Drool cascades over his three chins. He's trying to shove his flogger-whanger into the light socket! The drool runs over his sagging, hairy teats, flows in and out of the cellulite dimples of his monstrous gut and finally drips down onto his whanger-flogger and the light socket which electrocutes the sonofabitch and I think I'm gonna throw up!

"Can't we change the subject?" one of us asked, gagging.

We did.

But I don't know why we had to change the subject to me. I don't like to tell people too much about myself. It gives them ammunition. Especially this woman. She's too quick on the trigger as it is. Almost as bad as I am.

I gave her a condensed version of my plight out in Los Angeles, California. Stuck in a dead-end job, running around with deadhead people. I told her how I was supposed to have gone on my vacation with a group of the aforementioned deadbeats and, how, with bags packed and car loaded, I went into a state of panic and fled for New York with Morocco on my mind. Somewhere in relating all this to her, it dawned on me that my vacation had ended the day before and that I was then officially AWOL from my deadlocked job in a deadpan bank on deadly Wilshire Boulevard in deadass Los Angeles.

She told me she felt the same way about her job as a preschool teacher in Vancouver. The whole idea of taking the job had been to have enough free time to continue her education courses so that she could move up to a real teaching position, but it seemed like there just was never enough time to do much of anything . . . and that she had started to feel trapped. Trapped in that job. Trapped in Vancouver. Trapped in an affair that . . . that . . . "Oh forget it!" she said.

I gave her my best look of compassion, but I guess it wasn't convincing because she clammed up.

"How long have you been in Barcelona?" she asked.

You've got a lot of nerve, I thought, stopping as soon as you get to the good part and then expecting me to open up to you!

"I don't even know why I'm still in Barcelona," I complained. "I'm supposed to be somewhere, anywhere, in North Africa right now. I want to be in the land of camels, sand, oases and burnouses . . . burneese?"

"So go already," she said.

"I'm broke."

Something had gone awry with my best-laid plans. For one thing, I had stayed too long in New York. The plan called for two or three days stopover and I stayed for almost two months, but that's another story. Then there was the naive little dream about coming over on a freighter. I was only a decade or two too late for that scheme. Air fare bit hard into my reserves. And somehow I wound up in Luxembourg! I was supposed to be in Tangier or Gilbraltar . . . not Luxembourg! More money for train tickets. And the train stops in Paris. More money. Caught the flu or something, so more money to spend four days in Paris just trying to get rid of the malady . . . and Paris. Then Madrid and. . . .

"What's a burnous?" Stacey asked me.

I didn't know if I was boring her to death or if I had forgotten to speak out loud. I do that sometimes.

"Sort of like a robe, only you can wear it in public," I said. "Like a kaftan."

One of the things I like about the burnous, in comparison to the others, is that instead of pockets on either side, the burnous has slits so that you can reach inside to get into the pockets of your pants . . . or whatever, if you're not wearing anything underneath.

"How did you arrive at such a strange goal?" she asked.

"I think it started with this book I read years ago called *The Day on Fire*. It was a fictionalized version of the life of the poet Arthur

Rimbaud. Impressed the hell out of me. Depressed the hell out of me, too. But it did put some heavy romantic images in my mind."

"Sounds to me like you've been stalling a lot on your journey to the great desert. Second thoughts maybe?" She never rests . . . always on the attack. Witch.

"I told you I was broke," I protested.

"You weren't broke when you left Los Angeles. You spent your money not getting to Africa."

"Stacey, did I offend you in some manner so that you feel you have to get even with me?" I confronted, so unlike me.

"It's for your own good. You're never going to get there if you don't face your fears. What you have to do is. . . ."

I was walking alone in the desert. My *bota* was empty. My throat was parched. The hot sand burned through my worn sandals. My burnous was drenched with sweat. My vision was blurred to the point where even the mirages were out of focus. I was about to give up all hope of surviving when I spotted a speck on a far-off dune. A growing speck. It was a camel! It was a man on a camel, riding hell-bent-for-leather toward me. Rescue! It was . . . yes! . . . Günter!! He slowed his lumbering steed, reached for my outstretched hand and pulled me up behind him, and off we bounced toward Casablanca. I had to hold on to him to keep from falling off and when I put my hands on his hips, I noticed these two slits on either side of his burnous. I slipped my hands inside. The burnous was all he was wearing! Talk about your great rescues! I thought I was going to . . .

"Tad, are you listening to me?" She did it again, goddamnit!

"No, I'm not!" I was mad is what I was.

"May I have a cigarette?" she said softly. I was expecting a fight.

"What?!" I shouted, trying to stay on the offensive.

"May I please have a cigarette?" she repeated in her best feminine tones.

"Is this a trick?" Paranoia reigns.

"Tad."

I reached into my pocket, took out a pack and gave it to her.

"What are these? I thought you smoked Marlboros."

"I do. Oh sorry." I had given her my deadly, cough-enducing, stronger-than-shit, unfiltered, Spanish *cigarillos* which I keep around to give people who bum cigarettes. You flash a pack of Marlboros on the streets of Barcelona and fifty or sixty people converge on you from all parts of the city with their sad stories of why it is they don't have a cigarette on them and could they possibley borrow one. Borrow?! When the fuck do they plan to pay it back?! Nobody wants to borrow one of the Spanish ones. I wondered if my subconscious had deliberately made me pull out the nasty ones to give Stacey.

"You smoke these things?" she asked.

"Sometimes." I actually did from time to time. They weren't too bad if you didn't take big drags—sort of like the old Camels or Chester-fields, only soaked in horse piss and laid out to dry on the floor of a chicken coop in the summer.

"Are you okay?" Stacey asked. I sometimes get strange looks on my face. That must've been one of those times.

"I don't know. I don't know what I want. Maybe you're right about my being afraid to go to Africa. It is scary." What was scary was open-ing up to her. I knew I'd pay for it sooner or later, but I couldn't stop myself. "Courage has never been one of my strong suits. That book I was telling you about, the one about Rimbaud, deals a lot with hav-ing the courage of your difference. I haven't been able to get that part together yet. Like, what could I do down there without any money? I don't speak that language and I know nothing of their customs. I'd probably offend some sultan or emir and wind up castrated . . . or worse yet, married to one of their fat daughters."

"Maybe you'd get lucky and wind up married to one of their skinny sons," she jested cruelly, never missing an opportunity to jump on my vulnerability.

"Ha. Ha."

"Sorry."

"I think I don't go because I'm tired of being alone all the time. I'm afraid I'm going to end up alone forever at this rate."

"I'm here."

"For how long?"

"For now." She was serious.

"I need longer. And I need love, too. Romantic love."

"Sex," she surmised.

"There's nothing wrong with wanting sex, especially with love. I want a kindred spirit with . . ."

"A gorgeous body."

"Wouldn't hurt. But not essential. I want to look into his soul and for him to look into my soul. Is that asking so goddamn much?"

"It is a lot."

"Did you ever see the movie *Julia?*" I asked.

"Missed it."

"Too bad. It was great."

"Well?" she said when I dared pause long enough to swallow, breathe and light a cigarette. Stacey was into conversation and didn't tolerate a lot of pausing.

"I'm going. There's this terrific scene where Jane Fonda is sitting at a typewriter with a glass of whisky next to it and she can't get the words right . . . she's a writer . . . so she gets up and walks out the door and down onto the beach where she finds her lover, Jason Robards, who tells her that she should go have another glass of whisky and to keep writing until the words are right. That's what I want. I want to be a writer and I want a house on the beach, a typewriter with a glass of whisky next to it and a lover down on the beach who I can run to whenever the words aren't right."

"Is that all?"

"Not really. I would like to be wearing a white shirt, white pants, espadrilles and a straw hat."

"You are crazy." She was right.

"I know."

"You're putting too many requirements on your dream, Tad. Your recipe is too complicated."

"Oh, no," I muttered.

"It's like soup," she said with a straight face.

"This is going to be another food analogy, isn't it?" I asked.

"It doesn't matter what the ingredients are that go into the soup. What is important is the manual dexterity of the waiter who cleans it out of your lap!"

Good grief.

I think they asked us to leave. We were blitzed. I don't remember whether it was closing time or if we were misbehaving, but we were suddenly out in the street. Alone. In the middle of the night. Incapacitated.

There is something you should know about Barcelona's *Las Ramblas* at three in the morning. The bookstalls are all closed. The flower stalls are all closed. The street entertainers have all gone to wherever it is that street entertainers go at that hour. There are chalk drawings on the bricks – the humble offerings of young traveling artists who spend hours every day creating their masterpieces-for-pennies, only to have them washed away overnight.

We, Stacey and I, were unfortunately sitting in front of one of those masterpieces, admiring its rich textures and subtle colors, when the aforementioned washing away began that particular morning. Did I mention that the washing is done with fire hoses? It is. We were. Hosed.

They said they didn't see us sitting there. Shit, they're probably still laughing their asses off. Of course, we were laughing, too. That's what you call drunk – when you get propelled a block down *Las Ramblas* on a stream of water at three o'clock in the morning and think it's hilarious! Actually, it was a lot of fun. Akin to shooting the rapids if you're not an aficionado of that sport.

We dripped our way home.

"My *pensión's* just down another block," one of us said.

"Mine too," the other added. "We can slosh home together."

We were being exceptionally good sports about the whole thing.

"Anywhere near the *Pensión de las Flores*?"

"In it!"

"Me too!"

We were staying at the same *pensión*. Stacey and her traveling circus had just checked in that day and she had run right out to the docks to wave at ships and had met me and saw Günter and his Daddy and had dinner with a gypsy and a *sopa*-soaked *picha*, and had had too many drinks and had gotten hosed, so to speak, on Barcelona's famed *Las Ramblas* and had sloshed home with a drunken buddy right up to the front door of our mutually shared, quaint, little *Pensión de las Flores* and the fucking door was locked!

3. ¡Barthelona Thuckth!

Stacey and I both slept through breakfast. I suspect *La Familia* was cooking it as we dripped in earlier. Why else would they have all been up at 4:30 ayem? They weren't even pissed at us for coming home pissed and banging on their door at that ungodly hour. I mean the whole family was up and around to stare and giggle at our dampness. There was the señor and the señora *del Pensión de las Flores*, at least two if not three señoritas *del Pensión de las Flores*, and easily four señor juniors running around that place.

They clean. A lot. As in scrub with a bucket and brush. Everything. Everyday. Except Sunday. The whole city is like that. It's that employment thing I mentioned earlier. There are people who pick up trash off the streets and plazas all day long. There are those guys who play with fire hoses at night. There are people who attend to public restrooms and keep them clean and put out towels and accept mandatory tips. And there are whole families of people who run quaint little *Pensiónes de las Flores* for strange visitors from other countries who come banging on their doors in the middle of the night all wet.

Stacey and I stumbled, simultaneously, separately, into the dining room just before lunch was served. Her group was sitting at a table near the front window talking about us. At least I think they were talking about us. They acted as though they were talking about us. If I had been them, I would've been talking about us. I squinted at Stacey. I think she was wearing my glasses. I wasn't. We shuffled over to her friends.

She introduced me around the table, as they say. Dierdre and Biff—

strange couple. Mike and Toby—cute couple. And . . . and . . . the lech, señor supervisor, Mr. Up-Against-The-Wall-Muthafucka, old Slobber-Drool-Flogger-Whanger, himself! And you'll never guess what his name was! WALTER!!

"As in wall?" I thought I said to myself, but apparently not, because Dierdre blushed and eyed daggers at Stacey, who laughed.

Wall-ter wasn't really a slug, after all. Imagine if J. Edgar Hoover and Miss Piggy had an illegitimate son and you'd be seeing Wally. Abstractly repulsive. He looked like the type that wipes his nighttime boogers on the wall next to his bed.

What am I saying?! I used to do that myself! I was only eight at the time though. The Mother had decided that I should have bunk beds in my room just in case a sibling should happen to come along. (I don't know where the hell she thought it was going to come from!) Or in case I should ever want to ask one of my little friends over to spend the night with me. (Boy! If she only knew!) Anyway, I slept on the bottom bunk (fell off the top one six times the first week, so she made me sleep on the bottom one) and, given the dark nature of the lower depth of bi-level beds, I took to wiping my snot on the wall, knowing no one would ever see it. Wrong. The Mother, in one of her many whims, got the bright idea of taking the top bunk off and putting it on the floor next to the other one just like twin beds she said. God, what a mess! She was right; it was disgusting. She was so mad I thought she was going to make me lick it all off. Scraping, sanding and painting was ordered instead. So, I guess I should say that Wally Baby looked like the kind of adult that wipes his nighttime boogers on the wall next to his bed . . . and we'll just say that kids don't count.

Biff looked like he should be a salesman. He was a husky, good-looking, All-American Boy with just a trace of leftover baby fat. He had the kind of hair that changed from wavy to curly and back again depending on the time of day, the weather and his mood. He was one of those people who is so damn sure of himself when he has little or no reason to be. I knew I'd never be able to think of anything to say to him . . . ever.

Dierdre was the other half of the Ken and Barbie set. Susie Sorority, we always called her kind. Pert. Everything. She even had good posture. She had long, chestnut hair and could do a hundred different things with it, which she did regularly . . . usually with hair spray. Her lips were frozen in a permanent pout, even when she was generously sharing her tour guide smile.

Mike was cute. He was average height and build, a swimmer's body. He had dark hair and a little mustache, which I bet he groomed daily. He was the kind of person who would say "I beg your pardon" instead of "Huh?" like the rest of us.

Toby was taller than Mike and a little on the chubby side. He had sandy hair. He was probably the one Stacey meant when she said one of the gays in the group was effeminate, but he was nothing like the gypsy who had waited on us at the café. Unfortunately, Toby, when he wasn't being silly, was just the opposite of Biff—not at all sure of himself when, I thought, he had plenty of reason to be.

What a bunch we were, sitting at that table—each of us counting on Europe to be our salvation.

Wally was hoping the European female population would mistake that leer on his face for sensuality.

I was hesitantly pursuing my lofty dreams of Africa and burnous clad heroes.

Stacey was running from an affair and looking for some kind of cultural truth, whatever that is. When she wasn't selling magazines or playing with the group, she was haunting museums, galleries, churches, monuments and natural habitats, hoping to stumble onto some sort of spiritual enlightenment.

Mike and Toby said they were trying to save up enough money to open either a flower shop or antique boutique when they got back home, but what with the cost of cafés and nightclubs and new clothing, they had only been able to save $73 in the five weeks they'd been at the magazine game. There was something about their constant banter and the underlying tension between them that made me suspect they weren't on this trip just for money; maybe things hadn't been quite as wonderful as they had hoped in their relationship and they were expecting this European trip to bring them closer together. The magic of travel. A lot of straight couples try to save their marriages by having kids; gays travel.

Biff and Dierdre were in Europe looking for any vacant bed they could share and they were delighting in the fact that they had finally gotten away from her mother, who thought Biff was an empty-headed jockstrap interested in only one thing from her precious little girl. Damned perceptive woman, Dee's mom. But despite my revulsion at the thought of their coupling, they seemed to be the only ones among us with realistic goals. They had, in fact, already reached their goals— no mother and lots of sack time.

I wondered if I'd be able to get close to any of these people. They seemed as fucked up as the ones I'd run away from back in L.A. I was sure Stacey and I would be close. I was equally certain the opposite would be true for Ken and Barbie. I wasn't at all sure about MikenToby.

Ever notice how some names seem to go together? And how we often assign top billing to one or the other of the couple? Know why? It's usually because one way is easier to say than the other for us lazy-tongued Americans. To say MikenToby does not require a great deal of work inside the mouth. On the other hand, Toby-and-Mike, Toby-an-Mike or Toby-n-Mike all necessitate jaw, lip, tooth and tongue activity and the average person just ain't gonna put up with it. So, as long as Michael and Tobias remained a couple, they will undoubtedly be known as MikenToby.

Luncheon was served. *La Familia del Pensión de las Flores* entered en masse with piping hot platters piled high with fresh, steamed vegetables, hunks of bread and funny flat pieces of meat that were sitting off to the side emitting odors that were suspiciously liverlike.

"Ugh, liver!" Stacey groaned.

"*No señorita,*" one of *La Familia* corrected, "*es corazón.*"

"Thank you," Stacey politely responded and began eating.

So did the others. Eat. I guess I was the only one at the table who spoke any Spanish.

"Why aren't you eating, Tad?" Toby asked.

"I've always heard that when you eat heart, you should let it cool down first." It was very cruel of me to stress the word that way, but I didn't want anyone to miss it.

Gags around.

Stacey spit hers out on her plate which drew a scold from Dierdre who politely removed hers from her mouth with her napkin before she excused herself from the table followed closely by Biff who had given his piece of heart to Wally Baby who then wrapped it up with his own piece into his napkin and excused himself.

I couldn't help but wonder what he was going to do with those pieces of heart. I imagined him sitting on the edge of his bed up there in his room, dressed only in boxer shorts with little cupids on them, with one piece of heart on each of his jiggling jello-y thighs . . . and that's as far as I got. My mind wasn't in a disgusting enough mood at that moment and couldn't come up with anything worthy of Wally's tastes and talents.

Stacey and MikenToby ate their veggies and bread. I ate everything. Heart tastes like liver (blood is blood is blood). The only crisis came when I happened upon an inch-long cross section of an artery and they all threatened to leave the room if I didn't get rid of it instantly. I hid it under cigarette butts in the ashtray and they gave up smoking for the duration of the meal.

"Looks like you two had a wonderful time last night," Toby said.

How'd he know we were together? Like this: Dierdre and Stacey shared a room. Biff and MikenToby shared a room. Wally had his own room. We know why. Company policy dictated the boy-girl separation. They liked to pretend that their employees didn't fuck on the road. Biff should have been sharing with Wally, but Wally did the room assignments and wouldn't share, so he threw Biff in with the "boys." This also allowed Wally to pretend that MikenToby weren't fucking! But! Stacey's a wanderer, so she was seldom in her room which meant that Biff was which meant that he wasn't in with MikenToby which meant that they could. Anyway, at 4:30 that morning, Stacey staggered into the room, ejected Biff and tried to go to sleep. Unfortunately, Dierdre was awake and just had to get the details of our evening. Stacey wouldn't normally tell Dee everything, but Stacey was drunk and wet and tired and no match for Dierdre's probing questions. So Dee knew all and, of course, told all at breakfast that morning which Stacey and I had slept through. See?

Stacey and/or I grunted that we had had a good time.

"I like the part about the gypsy waiter!" Toby said. "Where is that café?"

"Never mind," said Mike with a lot more intensity than was called for at the moment.

"Never mind is right," I said. "That gypsy gave me nightmares this morning . . . morning mares?"

"Tell!" someone demanded.

I'm easy, so I did.

"Okay. I was sitting in this restaurant with a midget and I . . ." I began.

"Thanks," Stacey interrupted.

"It's a dream. Remember? Anyway, I had to go to the bathroom and someone directed me out the back door. There were those funny looking covered wagons all over the place. Gypsy wagons, I guess. Two huge transvestites grabbed me by the arms and . . ."

"How'd you know they were transvestites?" Mike challenged with just an edge of hostility in his voice. It was definitely meant for me and I sure didn't understand it.

"Hair. All over them. Well, maybe they weren't transvestites. I don't know. Will you leave me alone. They, the hairy ones, picked me up and put me into this giant vat of soup. Oh yeah, they ripped my clothes off first."

"A rape dream! How exciting!" Toby squealed in his best (worst?) girlish manner. Mike touched him on the arm. It must have been their private signal to butch it up.

"It wasn't a rape dream! They just tore off my clothes and threw me into the soup vat. Chicken vegetable, I think. But I wasn't the only live ingredient it turned out. Something very lobsterlike was pinching my penis!"

"No doubt the infamous six-legged African Peter Pinch," Toby instructed us.

"Wasn't he the actor who did *Network*?" asked Mike.

"Hymen!" Toby shouted.

"No!" Mike protested.

"Huh?" I asked.

"I call for a vote," Toby said.

"Huh?" I asked again.

All three of them tried to explain it to me at once. Seems as though MikenToby's jokes were getting so bad at times that they had to devise some form of punishment to discourage such flagrant abuses of humor, with puns usually being automatic grounds for punishment. But, either the accuser or the accused always had the right to call for a vote from the innocent victims of the joke. That time, Stacey and I were the only impartial victims, so we had to decide whether Mike got the Hymen, which was a cassette they had put together themselves featuring the world's oldest and worst jokes—a half-hour of them! H.Y.M.E.N. stood for: *H*enny *Y*oungman *M*eets *E*lsie *N*oosebaum.

"What if it's a tie?" I asked. "There are only two of us."

"Then the next joke is an automatic Hymen."

"Time to vote," said Toby.

"Hymen," Stacey voted.

I hesitated. Despite his unexplainable hostility toward me, he was a little cutie and I hated to do that to him.

"Be honest," Toby cautioned me. "Bad is bad."

"Please don't take all day," Mike jabbed.

"Hymen!" I blurted out in revenge.

Mike looked at me as though I had just confirmed his suspicions about my lack of character. Toby reached down beside his chair and lifted his knapsack to his lap. He took out one of those mini-portable-cassette-players-with-headphones and handed it to Mike who put it on. The rules stated that the condemned person serve his(er) sentence on the spot. Poor Mike had to sit there at the table and listen to that tape for thirty minutes while watching us have a good time, our muted mouths moving. He was grimacing and my heart went out to him. I could've sworn there were tears in his eyes at one point. I was so glad when it was over.

I tried to get it out of my mind by getting back to ol' jello-thighs up in his room with the pieces of broiled heart, but my heart wasn't in it. Hymen! I think it had something to do with flies, but before I had time to figure it out, a fireman appeared on the fire escape just outside the window. It was Günter! The building was on fire and he was the only fireman available that day because all the others were home with the flu or something. He needed my help to rescue all the women and children in the building. He said it was okay to leave Wally right where he was. I agreed to help, assuming we'd save everyone and then go down the street for a few beers so he could thank me . . . properly. We . . .

"Let's go," Stacey said.

Damn I hate it when people interrupt. But I forgave her that time because Mike looked like he needed to go out for some fresh air. His eyes were glazed. That Hymen must be strong stuff, I thought.

Outside. Barcelona is bigger than you probably think it is, if you ever thought about it at all. Anyway, it is a sprawling hub—a giant wheel extending its spokes for miles in every direction out from the city center, which is in the center. We were at the end of one of those spokes, *Las Ramblas*, near the harbor, the sailor district, the red-light district, the hustler district. In other words, the fun part of the city. The area was seething with dope, whores, booze, killers and wide-eyed innocents such as ourselves who thought they were sufficiently sophisticated to be running around in such a sleazy place.

The fifth fleet of the United States Navy docked in that harbor and, believe me, when that happened there wasn't a clean knee in the town.

"Is that what they mean when they say Barthelona Thuckth?" Toby asked.

"I don't think so," I told him. "And shouldn't that be a Hymen?"

"You can't call Hymens," Stacey said. "It has to be either Mike or Toby." The phrase screwed, blewed and tattooed was invented in Barcelona.

"Are you gay?" Mike asked me. I guess Stacey didn't tell Dierdre everything about our night together.

"Let's just say that, at this phase of my life, my *dis*preference has swung to the female side," I hedged.

"I beg your pardon?" Mike said. See what I meant about him? Polite.

"I believe that people are instinctively bisexual and are taught or traumatized into avoiding sexual relationships with one gender or the other. Monosexual's don't choose which way they go—they go the way they learned to dislike. Hence, a dispreference rather than a preference."

I try not to spout off like that with new friends, but we were, at that moment, on our second round of drinks in our third bar for the afternoon, turning that morning's hangover into tomorrow's. It was Saturday. They didn't have to start selling magazines until Monday morning.

We were in my favorite bar. It wasn't that the bar was nicer than other bars in the area, but I had made a friend in that one. Her name was María. She worked behind the bar during the day and "worked the bar" at night. She was sort of a mother figure there—the other 'girls' looked to her for advice and no one messed with her. She liked me. No one messed with me because they knew they'd catch hell from María. When I was alone, she'd buy me drinks. I even used to give her my Marlboros when I walked in and she would dole them out to me while I was there, pretending they were hers. No one would ask her for one.

María was off the afternoon that Stacey, MikenToby and I were there drinking. I would've liked to introduce them. Maybe not. Very often the people I like don't like each other. I can't give parties.

We finished our drinks and went to a movie. *The Sound of Music*. In Spanish. Not subtitled. Dubbed! All the songs were in Spanish. Except "Do Re Mi." Doe a deer doesn't make sense in translation. Ditto a drop of golden sun, a long long way to run and a needle pulling thread. The film was old and scratched and faded and the voices they used to dub it were awful and the theater smelled and the popcorn was chewy and we had a wonderful time!

We went to a few more bars, then all-night cafés, then morning and afternoon movies—Spanish movies in Spanish so that we couldn't understand them. They spoke too fast for me and when I did get a few words here and there and tried to translate them for my friends, everybody went "Shhh!" All over the theater. Then more bars. And lots of yapping.

It turned out the whole group was from the Vancouver area. Toby had moved there from San Francisco after he met Mike, but everyone else in the group had grown up there. It was kind of a weird weekend for me in that I wasn't used to being around such open people. They actually said what was on their minds and told stuff that most of us would even have trouble telling a shrink or a priest.

Like on Saturday morning when we were sitting in an alley somewhere eating herring out of a can and sharing a brick of cheese and a bottle of wine (wine, by the way, which would give Ripple a run for its money) and Stacey started chatting about her affairs with married men, in graphic detail, and about how she used to get blitzed in hotel bars and wake up in some guy's room the next morning and how she thought it must've had something to do with the way her father had always ignored her or at least had not shown her affection. When she had mentioned earlier that she'd had affairs with married men, I'd assumed she meant the discreet kind of affairs you see in the movies. Not bed-hopping! I should've guessed the day I met her, when she was nagging me about being afraid of commitment, that she'd had firsthand experience along those lines.

Then on Saturday afternoon, when we were all lying stretched out on these huge boulders down by the sea, eating raw carrots and some kind of pita bread, Toby unashamedly told us about how he'd cured his bed-wetting problem just before they'd all come over to Europe and how he'd taken his very last wet sheet and hidden it in the back of his father's closet behind some boxes to show the sonofabitch exactly how he felt about the years of humiliation he'd felt because of his old man's taunting over that selfsame bed-wetting.

I wish I had that kind of nerve.

Mike was funny about our confession sessions. All weekend he talked about what wonderful parents he had and how much he had enjoyed his childhood, but he told his stories in such a way as to make them sound like he was revealing deep dark secrets . . . just to keep the confessional mood flowing. I think the most astounding revelation he made was that he once lied to his mother about the true ownership of the muscle magazine she'd found in his underwear drawer. Wicked boy.

In spite of the mutual trust atmosphere they had set up, I had great difficulty in opening up. I wanted to tell them how grateful they should be to have fathers at all and how lucky they were not to be afraid of their mothers, but I told them about Teddy Bear Sam instead.

On Sunday afternoon, (I think it was right after one of our movies and we were drinking Pepsis at a little cantina with Italian umbrellas all over its patio), MikenToby got into a squabble over whether or not gays should or even could be Christians. They'd had a half-dozen minor scraps already that day, but that one got nasty. I did my best to stay out of it, remembering the number of friends I'd lost in the past after religious discussions and how futile such arguments are anyway. Stacey seemed to be doing the same.

I'm not sure how we managed to get started on religion in the first place, but I think it came out of the resolution that Wally was going to, or should if there really was one, burn in hell. Yeah, that was it because then Mike said something about how that was probably why humans invented the concept of eternal damnation — to console themselves that the so-called bad guys in this life would eventually have to pay for their misdeeds.

Toby jumped on that "invented" crack and the big debate was on. Toby was already upset because the minister at the church he'd been attending in Vancouver had sermonized against homosexuality — or at least it seemed that way to Toby — and he was considering switching to the gay church when they got back home.

"How can there be such a thing as a gay church?" Mike served.

"Why not?" Toby returned.

"Because Christians think that homosexuality is an abomination against God! That's why!"

"Not all Christians think that!" Toby shouted.

"Well the Church does and how can you walk into a church that thinks you're an abomination?"

"The gay church doesn't think that way!" Toby said.

"Don't they use the Bible?"

"Sure they use the Bible."

"Then they're hypocrites!"

"I don't care what you say, I believe that gays can and should be Christians," Toby whined.

"Why? Because your mother said you had to?"

"No!" Toby blurted out. I could feel the hurt.

"You know, Toby," Mike said, "some people actually think for themselves rather than believe everything other people tell them."

"You're full of shit!" Toby screamed.

"And you suck cock behind the altar!" Mike said.

See what I mean? Futile.

"Hey guys," I got involved against my better judgment, "don't you think this is just an exercise in masturbation?"

"God! Are you all atheists?" Toby bellowed.

"I didn't say I was an atheist," I said. "I just think arguments about religion are useless."

"Are you an atheist?" Toby demanded.

"I don't want to get into this," I told him.

"You are an atheist," he accused.

"Useless!" I shouted.

Stacey jumped in at that point. "I like the feeling I get when I'm sitting in a church." She took Toby by the arm and walked away from Mike and me. "There's something about the atmosphere. I think it's hope that I feel. Not necessarily for myself, but just the fact that hope does exist somewhere in this world, this life, and . . . ."

Mike paid the check and we followed them at a safe distance. We stopped for another round of drinks.

We were still drunk when we got back to the *pensión*. It was dinner time. We were bad. We teased and taunted the hell out of Dierdre and Biff. Wally left in disgust before dessert. I didn't actually witness him doing it, but I suspected that he took his dessert up to his room with him. MikenToby were so bad that they each got three Hymens, which they promised to do as soon as they got back to their room. We were having too much fun at the time to allow them to do their Hymens on-the-spot, as the rules stated.

I didn't know why Biff and Dierdre were putting up with us, but they did seem more relaxed than usual. It may have had something to do with the fact that they had had a room all to themselves for two days while the rest of us were out misbehaving. Bee and Dee even got into our game of Deserted Island.

I've always found Deserted Island to be one of the more interesting group games. It can be so revealing. But you can't start it out as a game. You have to sneak into it slowly. You wait for someone in the group to express dissatisfaction with the way our society is these days and then you say something stupid like, "Wouldn't it be great if we could get away from it all, just the five, six, seven of us?" Someone will pick it up from there and the game is on. Once it's moving well, you can step in and explain how the discussion can be played as a game. If you're up to keeping score in your head, you don't have to tell them it is a game until it's over, but I was too far gone to keep score by myself, so I had to clue them in up front. The group votes on each move by each player to determine how many points (s)he gains or loses.

Some highlights of our game that night:

We gave Biff and Dierdre 200 points each just for agreeing to play with us. I figured they'd need a handicap anyway.

Mike got 25 points for wanting to take the collected works of Proust.

Dierdre lost 50 points for wanting to take the works of Harold Robbins.

Toby lost a 100 for wanting to take thirty years of Readers Digest Condensed Books.

Mike gained 50 for asking if he could bring his cassettes of Beethoven's sonatas.

Toby lost 25 points on Johnny Mathis.

Stacey scored a 100 points for offering to learn Beethoven's sonatas on the flute.

Biff lost 50 because he wanted to take one of those new battery-powered TVs.

I lost 25 for saying I thought we should ask the rock group Queen to meet us there. I could have made room for them in my hut.

In the clothing area, Stacey scored 25 for suggesting we could all wear loincloths and/or some kind of wrap-arounds.

Dee lost 25 just for saying "cashmere."

Mike got 25 for wanting to become a nudist. I said he should've gotten 50, but the others overruled me.

Toby lost 25 for objecting to Mike being naked in front of the group.

Biff lost 25 because he wanted Dierdre to become a nudist, but not him.

In the category of love interest, we gave Biff and Dierdre and Miken-Toby 25 points each for being content with their present couplings.

I lost 25 for suggesting we practice free love and another 25 for wanting to call Jack Wrangler to see if he was available.

Stacey gained 50 for saying she wouldn't mind being celibate if she could dedicate the rest of her life to the study and contemplation of life-in-general, but we took it away from her when she admitted that if we were all that was available, she would just as soon do without anyway.

Biff and Dierdre were awarded 50 points each for agreeing to have four children to keep our island populated.

MikenToby also got 50 each for agreeing to have children. After all, it's the thought that counts.

Stacey scored 50, too, by agreeing to have kids by one of the gay men. Biff couldn't father Stacey's children because they wouldn't be able to mate with the kids he had with Dierdre—half-siblings I guess they would be.

We took Biff's 50 points away from him for pretending not to understand that.

I lost 50 and got clobbered on the arm for suggesting we take vials of sperm from Wally to artifically inseminate Stacey.

We played for what seemed like hours and when the game finally ended for want of sleep, we awarded the bonuses and tallied the scores:

Dierdre got a negative bonus of 50 points for saying she was just pretending to be interested in the game.

Biff also got a minus bonus because he got so involved in the game that he was disappointed that we weren't really going to go.

MikenToby each got a 50 point bonus for pledging to be happy anywhere they were as long as they could be together.

Stacey got 25 points for thinking that we might be able to do something like this in the future, even though we weren't able to do it now. You can't punish hope.

I was penalized 100 points for getting so involved in the game that I was disappointed we weren't really going—when I was the idiot who started the damn game in the first place!

Mike won with a whopping 1250 points! Stacey was a very close second, then Toby, Dierdre, Biff and, finally, me with a minus 10! I went to bed.

4. Hello Columbus!

O the sweet smells of a summer night, walking up the world's longest plaza.

"Hola Cesar."

Millions of flowers lifted their aromatic voices in harmony along *Las Ramblas.*

"Guten nacht Ernst."

Diesel. A Mercedes whizzed by on one of the crowded, narrow roads that flank the walkway.

"Bon soir Alain."

Chicken feathers? I imagined a robust, sweating señorita plucking away at a robust, sweating stew hen up on the third floor above me. In an hour, the smell would be very different. I promised myself to wander back down that way later.

"Hiya Jack."

Now, what's that smell? I thought. Fish? Octopus? Peasant soup maybe. No, just a garbage can, stupid.

"Hey Stanislaus."

All the bums were out on the plaza. They always were on the balmy nights.

Try this on for size: You're somewhere between seventeen and thirty. You're not ready to settle into a job yet. And you're out to see the world with your thumb up and your hand out. There must've been hundreds of them in Barcelona that summer . . . from all over the world.

I had met guys from England, Ireland, Germany, Switzerland, Finland, South America, and a few places I'd never even heard of.

No women. I remember seeing a few women who were street entertainers, but none among the bums.

There was a loose code you were supposed to follow. You weren't asked to share your money or drag another bum along if you were getting treated to a meal, but you were expected to share things like cigarettes and grass. They also pooled information on good places to hang out for the best hand out and on any large groups that happened to be in town at the moment. Everyone watched out for newcomers and introduced them around, letting them know the rules and so on.

These bums were generally courteous, sober and clean when-it-was-possible. Because they didn't cause any trouble, the locals and the tourists were fairly generous. Sometimes in the form of cash; other times perhaps a hamburger, a cup of coffee, a full meal or a drink. Sometimes sex was requested, but usually not. About half the guys would do it if someone asked; the others wouldn't. Some of those who would do it would do it only with women; others only with men; and others didn't care about gender at all. But, like I said, sex was seldom required or even mentioned. No one ever mentioned it to me.

I didn't go out bumming very often, but it was an excellent means of stretching the little bit of money I had left. I couldn't sing or play an instrument or draw with chalk on sidewalks . . . and foreigners weren't allowed to work by law . . . so bumming was about the only alternative.

The best stint I remember came to about forty pesetas, a three-course meal and two drinks.

The worst time I remember came to two pesetas, one fast-food-type hamburger and a two-hour conversation with an Englishman who insisted on talking about his wife's vagina and yielded me one watered-down rum and Pepsi.

Anyway, the Monday after our big weekend, Stacey and Group had to get to work selling magazine subscriptions and I hit *Las Ramblas* in an attempt to get together some room-and-board money.

Within an hour I had run into a dozen bums I knew already and had met a dozen new ones who had appeared since the last time I ventured out onto the plazas.

Someone asked to "borrow" a cigarette and I said something dumb like "oh sure" and reached into my pocket, smug in the knowledge that this was only going to cost me one or two nasty, deadly, cough-enducing, stronger-than-shit, unfiltered, Spanish *cigarillos*. Guess which moron pulled out an unopened pack of Marlboros! You never saw so many hands in your life!

One of those hands was left holding my empty pack of Marlboros. There was a small tatoo on the back of that hand; it was a dragon. I looked up to ask the dragon's owner if it meant anything, but my mouth wasn't working. The dragon belonged to Günter!

"Hi," I said quietly. Hi?! Is that all you have to say? I thought. Here was this gorgeous blond hunk with whom I'd done battle in Bavaria, with whom I'd ridden on a camel across the desert with my hands in his burnous and with whom I'd rescued people from a burning building . . . and what did I say? Hi.

"Hi," is what he said too, but he had an excuse—he didn't know any of that had happened.

We went through the usual, awkward moments of trite and polite small talk. I hate that. People should be more like dogs—one or two well-placed sniffs and it's over. I offered him one of the Spanish cigarettes. He actually took it . . . and smoked it! So naturally, I had to have one, too.

I was fairly certain he didn't remember me and I was getting antsy trying to keep up our friendly little chat. Finally, I just couldn't take it any more and blurted out:

"What happened to your rich friend?" Now, at first, that question doesn't look so bad, but you should've heard the inflections. There was innuendo, insinuation, insidiousness, inanity, inappropriateness, insensitivity, incautiousness, incendiarism, indecency and inquisition. I was ashamed.

"Who?" Günter asked.

"The old man you were with on the boat!" I was a brazen hussy is what I was.

"Were you with a little red-haired girl?"

Oh great! He remembers Stacey! Yeah, asshole, I was the beige sack of shit standing next to her!

"Yes," is what I said, shyly. I knew one of us was being a nerd and I didn't think it was him . . . or is it he? Why was I worrying about grammar at such an emotional moment?

He didn't have much of an accent at all. I guess those German schools teach good English. He was quite fluent in fact, with only rare lapses into his native tongue. I'd like to lapse into his native tongue, I thought.

"You want to walk up the hill?" Günter asked.

"What's the hill?" I asked, just to be conversational. I'd've followed him up the side of Mount Everest if he asked.

"You'll see. Come on."

I made a mental note to myself that he didn't answer my question about the man who was with him on the boat.

The road wound around the hill in a sloping spiral, each circular lap growing smaller as we neared the crest. It seemed like a long walk to me and I was trying to remember if you could calculate the running length of a spiral if you knew the radius, but it occurred to me that I'd probably have to know the angle of the slope as well. I didn't know the angle of the slope. Hell, I didn't know the radius either. So I gave up and decided simply that it was a very long walk. It must've taken us an hour and a half to get to the top. I had to guess at the time because I didn't have a watch with me. Earlier in the evening, I had thought I had my trusty new LCD $2.98 pen watch, but when I pulled it out to check the time, it said, "Dixon Ticonderoga 1388-2 Soft." Günter looked at me funny, but he didn't say anything. Europeans think Americans are strange anyway.

At the top there was this huge fortlike structure, a monument to someone famous in Spanish history whose name I didn't notice at the time because I had other things on my mind. I remember you could see the whole city from up there and that the view was inspiring. I was inspired to talk.

I told him my frustrations at home, my dreams of Africa, my visions of being a writer on a beach somewhere (I left out the part about the lover), my financial troubles and my funny story about the German couple I sat next to on the plane from New York to Luxembourg. I thought, being German, he'd be sure to see the humor in it. You see, the three of us were seated together—me on the aisle, the husband in the middle and the pregnant wife next to the window. She didn't want to drink alcohol, so he and I split hers. Two complete dinners were served on this flight, each with two complimentary cocktails, two glasses of wine and one glass of brandy. Twice we did this, sharing her portion. At high altitude. Schnockered. He spoke some English; she didn't. From the time we took off, she called him Schatz. Schatz this, Schatz that. Had to be his name, right? So that's what I called him. Schatz. I found out later that *Schatz* means dear, sweetheart, honey or whatever endearment you like. I was so embarrassed. They never said a word. What they must've thought of me. He was kind of cute.

Back to Günter. After a couple of hours, I finally shut up, realizing I was doing all the revealing and that I wasn't learning anything about him. I cautiously asked again about the man on the boat, a little apprehensive about what the answer might be. I needn't have worried—he changed the subject without answering. Again.

The subject was changed to sex. Now I know that guys are supposed to sit around late at night talking about sex, comparing conquests and all that bullshit, but no way did I want to get into that with him.

It wasn't too bad as it turned out. Most of it was pseudophilosophical stuff and, thus, vague. He didn't say so exactly, but he seemed to want me to get the impression that he was bisexual. He worked in a couple of well-placed vagaries about the man on the boat, William, and about a woman he knew named Pamela. Both rich. Both English. Both in Barcelona.

He seemed to be saying that he believed sexual activity needed to be administered with restraint and with much forethought. One shouldn't be lying around indiscriminately or with abandon. Gay abandon they used to call it. I thought he was a little too calculating, but he was right in a way. One needn't be promiscuous. A little sexual restraint is good. I can do that. My problem is that I get it all worked out intellectually, then I don't know what to do with my dick.

Speaking of which, mine was misbehaving again. My imagination had started to take off on its own while we were talking: There were thirty cannon surrounding the fort. Günter and I were the only survivors of a bloody massacre by the French. (Why do I have so many military fantasies? I hate the military!) Günter was wounded in the thigh and I had to get the bullet out to save his life! I ripped his pants off and, at great personal sacrifice, lowered my mouth to his wound. Wound! I said. I sucked feverishly and manipulated the bullet with my tongue until I had it worked up . . . to the surface of the skin. Then I bit it!

Oh shit! I thought, here I am sitting with the guy, in the flesh so to speak, and I still can't stop fantasizing about him. I wondered why I had switched victim/hero roles with him in my daydreams. I tried to conceal my excitement from him, but he had seen it. He just smiled.

The sun was also rising, so we started back down the hill. I babbled on about sunrises, sunsets, sloping spirals, sand dunes — anything to keep my mind from straying back to his wound. The flush wouldn't leave my face.

We separated somewhere along *Las Ramblas* and I made a beeline for the *pensión* and bed.

I had a dream.

I was bebopping along the beach, minding my own business, when these twin Amazons came up to me and asked if they could borrow my cock. Not me, mind you, just the genitalia. I think they might have been lesbians. I didn't want to loan my cock to them, so I said I didn't have one. They both pointed at it. I looked down and discovered to my horror that I was stark naked! Right there on . . . on whatever beach that was. And it wasn't a nudist beach either because everyone else was dressed. I mean dressed! There were two couples down by the water and the women were wearing granny dresses. The men had on formal evening gowns . . . in the middle of the day! Two little girls over by the swings wore red, white and blue pinafores and the lifeguard was modeling a stunning off-the-shoulder floor-length slit-up-to-the-thigh pale pink hostess frock by Dior. It was dazzling. One of the Amazon sisters was in a frilly summer dress and carried a parasol. The other was in leather and chains and carried a whip, which she offered to snap my cock off with if I didn't want to give it up freely. So I gave in. I don't know how I thought I was going to disconnect everything, but I never got the chance to find out. When I reached down there, I discovered the most ghastly thing I've every seen in my life! Extending down from the groin, there was this huge cavity in my thigh! The opening was eight or nine inches long and about three inches wide. My leg was hollow! And inside that hideous hole was this dripping, brown, sticky goo! I got hysterical! I was screaming and shaking and trying to force the hole closed with my hands, terrified that I might get some of that deadly goo on them. The leathered twin slapped me across the face and I started crying. The frilly twin stepped in and gently wiped the tears from my eyes, telling me in the most soothing tones that there wasn't a hole in my leg at all, that it was just a silly old glob of peanut butter. No it's not! I know it's a hole! I cried. She told me not to be such a silly little boy and that she was going to get that nasty old peanut butter off my leg so that it wouldn't scare her little Tadpole anymore. She dropped to her knees and starting licking the inside of my thigh. I lost it. Completely.

I also woke up. Damn!

I showered, dressed and ran downstairs. No one was around, so I fixed myself a snack and took it back up to my room. Shortly there was a knock at the door.

It was Günter.

Come for a quick fuck did you, hot stuff? is what I wanted to say.

"Hi," is what I said. "Want part of a peanut butter sandwich?"

He declined.

"They're not back yet," I said, meaning MikenToby and Stacey. I had invited Günter to join us for the evening, but they weren't back yet.

"What do you want to do?" he asked.

Don't do this to me, God.

"I dunno. Whatayou wanna do?" I can be very articulate at times.

"I could use some more sleep. Mind if I stretch out here for a while?" he asked.

Get thee behind me, Satan.

"Naw, go ahead," I said. I'll just bind and gag myself and writhe on the floor while you sleep.

"Are you sure you don't mind?"

"No, not at all," I said. Lie down you sonofabitch! I want to slobber in your crotch!

He started to take off his clothes, when some no-good, traitorous, treacherous, ass-sucking, piss-drinking, shit-eating motherfucker knocked on the door.

I know I must've whimpered out loud.

"We're back!" Stacey yelled from the other side of my door.

"Terrific!" I yelled back as Günter started to put his clothes back on. "You can go ahead and rest for a while if you want," I told him. "They probably want to freshen up anyway."

"We shouldn't keep them waiting," he said, reverting to some useless etiquette he probably learned from those rich assholes he lives off of. I'm gonna kill someone for this. I swear.

"They can wait!" I shouted. I'm not usually that aggressive when I'm sober.

"Come on, Tad, let's go," he said and out the door he went.

I slammed it behind him and locked it!

Knock. Knock.

"What?"

"Tad?"

"What?!"

"What are you doing?"

"Nothing."

"Come out."

"You wanted to go with them so goddamn much! Go!"

"What is wrong with you?"

"Nothing."

"Open the door."

"No."

"They are not here."

"Whataya mean they're not there?"

"There is no one out here."

"I don't believe you."

"Look for yourself."

"I will."

I opened the door slowly. Something hit it like a battering ram, landing on top of me as I was smashed to the floor. It was Günter.

"Hi," I said.

"Are you ready to go?" he asked.

Lying on top of me was one hundred and seventy-five pounds of fantasy-come-to-life. I was definitely ready to go!

"Oh yeah," I moaned, looking up into those blue-blue eyes.

"*Gut*," he said and pulled me up by the arm and out into the hall. Oh well.

He was telling the truth—there wasn't anyone in the hall. We found them in Stacey's room.

"Gesundheit!" she said.

"Gesundheit!" MikenToby said.

Dierdre and Biff were polite.

Wally was . . . wherever.

Günter asked me later why my friends had said Gesundheit! when I introduced him to them. I made up something about how they probably thought they should speak to him in German, his being German, just to be friendly and that Gesundheit! was probably the only word they could remember at the moment.

First, we went to the bar where María worked because I wanted María to meet them and vice versa. She wasn't particularly impressed with them and vice versa. I vowed never to introduce my friends to each other again. We ran out of there quickly when someone spotted Wally towards the back of the bar with a teenage hooker on each arm.

Then we went to *La Guitarra*. That was some bar! There must have been five or six different levels in the place—all with open staircases and railings so that you could see all the way to the back and all the way up to the ceiling. It gave you the feeling of scaffolding, only much stronger. A problem was that they only served wine. We started with a pitcher of dry red. A large pitcher of dry red.

With our second large pitcher of wine, MikenToby introduced us to one of their favorite games, TV Sitcom. There are no assigned roles; you just have to be creative and jump in whenever you can. Mike started:

FADE IN.

> MIKE/WARD
> Oh June! I'm home!
>
> TOBY/JUNE
> Ward, we have to talk about the Beaver.
>
> DIERDRE
> I was going to be Mrs. Cleaver! I knew what show it was!
>
> TOBY
> Whoever's first gets the part.
>
> STACEY AS THE BEAVER
> Hi Mom. Hi Dad. Have you seen Wally?
>
> MIKE/WARD
> Beaver, your mother and I have to talk with you.
>
> DIERDRE
> Why does she get to be the Beaver?
>
> MIKENTOBY
> Because she was first!
>
> DIERDRE
> Well, who can I be then?
>
> MIKE
> That's part of the game; you have to figure it out.
>
> DIERDRE
> Then I don't want to play.
>
> ALL
> Then don't!

TAD/WALLY
Hi Mom. Hi Dad. Hiya, Beav.

STACEY/BEAVER
Oh hi, Wally.

DIERDRE
Damn it!

TOBY
Dierdre, you can be Eddie Haskell.

DIERDRE
But he was a creep!

We all just looked at her . . . not a word.

DIERDRE (CONT'D)
Biff, take me home!

BIFF
Shut up, Deedee, and drink your wine!

She did.

TAD
Let's start over. Okay?

MIKE/OZZIE
Oh Harriet! I'm home!

TAD
Could we possibly do something newer?

STACEY
I agree.

MIKE/RICKY
Oh Lucy! I'm home!

ALL
No!!

MIKE/ARCHIE
Oh Edith! I'm home!

GÜNTER
Do all American television shows start the same way?

ALL
Yes!

STACEY/EDITH
Oh Archieeeeeee!

Stacey grabbed Mike and kissed him a half-dozen times.

MIKE/ARCHIE
Can you wait'll I get my jacket off, Dingbat?

DIERDRE/GLORIA
Hi, Daddy. How was work today?

MIKE/ARCHIE
Terrific Gloria! Everyone sit down and I'll tell you all about it.
Where's the beer, Edith? Gloria! Not in my chair! And I'm only
going to tell this once, so go get that Pollack husband of yours.

DIERDRE/GLORIA
Daddeeeeeee!

MIKE/ARCHIE
Where is the meathead?

Without meaning to, we all looked at Biff.

BIFF
Hey! No way! C'mon Deedee, let's go!

DIERDRE
Shut up and drink your wine!

He did.

MIKE/ARCHIE
Where's the meathead?

GÜNTER
Sein Arschloch ist zugeschnappt!

STACEY
What?

TOBY
Who are you supposed to be?

GÜNTER
I am their German neighbor, Fritz.

MIKE
They didn't have a German neighbor, Fritz.

TAD
Who cares? What did you say?

GÜNTER
I said he died.

STACEY
The meathead is dead?

MIKE
Tell them what it really means.

GÜNTER
It is not polite.

MIKE
It means his asshole snapped shut!

FADE OUT

Around the third or fourth pitcher of wine, we decided that I should call my friend María at the bar and ask her to play a little joke on

Wally. Trouble was we couldn't think of anything rotten enough to do to him.

Günter saved the day. He suggested we ask María to tell the girls to take Wally to *El Lagorto Rosado*, The Pink Lizard! (And Günter hadn't even met Wally-the-creep yet!) I wondered how Günter knew about the strange place, but then I'd heard of it and so had MikenToby. We had to explain it to Stacey.

The Pink Lizard was a bar over in the roughest part of the harbor district. The patrons of the bar specialized in Attitude Readjustment for homophobes and other such asshole-types as Wally. Whores often took Johns there if the guy roughed them up or tried to stiff them for the fee. The place was loaded with some of the prettiest (in the dark) women you could find in Barcelona. Only they weren't women. And they weren't your everyday drag queens either. What they were was the meanest bunch of sadists and rapists you could ever hope to find in one place, each with a fetish for so-called virgins.

Normally, I wouldn't approve of such violent means, but in my drunken state it seemed like a perfect evening out for old Wally Baby. I made the call.

Around the fifth or sixth pitcher of dry red wine, the whole joint was singing . . . and not just in Spanish. Each table, or any group of nationals, could choose a song in any language (we chose the Mouseketeer Song) and the rest of the mob was supposed to follow along. Somehow. I swear we were singing in languages none of us spoke.

Around the seventh or eighth pitcher of dry red wine, it wasn't dry red wine. It was sangría! Sweet, sickening sangría. That did it. Sugar. Fruit juices. Sickness.

Biff and Dierdre didn't even get through their first glass of the stuff before they had to leave. Either MikenToby puked before the rest of us could get down the steps out in front of the bar. Whichever one of the two wasn't throwing up held the other one's head and cleaned him up and then we all staggered down *Las Ramblas* toward the harbor.

They have, in Barcelona, a full-size reproduction of Columbus' flagship, the Santa María. If you want to call that pint-sized boat full-size. It was though. Ships were tiny in those days. I don't know how all those men slept in there. They must've been in love. If they weren't when they left Spain, they probably were by the time they reached the new world.

We sneaked aboard. The only guard system provided the shrine at night was local pride — the old honor system, which says that everyone is supposed to care enough about something to follow the rules without being forced to. Drunks at three in the morning have no pride.

Our self-guided tour didn't last very long. There wasn't very much to see. We collapsed on the deck to finish off the pitcher of wine Stacey had carried out of the bar. I don't remember if it was the dry or the sweet red. I don't think I could tell at that moment, actually.

Stacey took one swig out of the pitcher and threw up on the steering wheel, or whatever you call that thing. The last we saw of her that night she was running up *Las Ramblas* toward the *pensión*, waving the wine pitcher and shouting "*Toro!*"

Without wine to fortify us, we sort of fizzled out and started looking for a place to sleep. We stumbled onto two useable bunks downstairs . . . below.

MikenToby fell into one of the bunks and commenced billing and cooing and petting.

Günter fell into the other. I hesitated for one or two seconds, then crawled in next to him. He was going to have to eject me physically if he didn't want me there. I was that drunk. He didn't.

He stretched out on his back with his hands behind his head. I nestled cautiously onto his shoulder, hoping he wouldn't push me away. Again he didn't. God this is nerve-racking!

He adjusted his arm under my neck and around my shoulders. I stopped breathing, I think.

Somehow my free hand wound up on his belly, ready to leap away at the first sign of resistance. Nothing. Now, I was perfectly happy with the way things were — I could've stayed like that forever — but my hand got impatient and wanted to go wandering off to more adventurous territory. It did. He said nothing. He just lifted my hand from his crotch and placed it back on his belly.

I passed out.

5. Your Father Wears Espadrilles!

I was, understandably, sailing with Columbus on the Santa María. The ship was, strangely, carrying harpoons. I was, weirdly, playing the part of Tom Sawyer, but they called me Arschficker. (*Arschficker* is a German word which means exactly what it looks like it means.) "Call me Arschficker", I wrote in my little notebook.

I was a cabin boy. My Aunt Polly had sold me to them for the voyage. The first day went pretty well as I ran around trying to learn my duties, but that night they brought out this barrel and told me I was supposed to get in it. Captain Chris said every ship had to have a boy-in-the-barrel to keep the sailors from getting mean on long voyages. From my experience, I can tell you sailors get mean even when there is a boy-in-the-barrel on ship. I had just gotten to sleep, crouched up in that smelly barrel, when they started banging on it and cursing like the devil himself! They tore that strong, handcrafted barrel apart in seconds! Just to get at me! They were about to do something with ropes to me when Captain Chris came in and saved me. He told me I had to be good to the sailors or they'd probably throw me overboard and that he didn't want a mutiny on his ship so I'd damn well better get to it! Being good to the sailors meant that they got to pass me around from bunk to bunk every night and on Sunday afternoons. Let me tell you that, from what I saw, they didn't need me at all — they were being good to each other all over the place.

Everybody, that is, except the one they called the Viking. He always stayed to himself. He was clean and really handsome. The others were all dirty, smelly and double ugly. I started thinking that all this wouldn't be so bad if I could be with him. I saved all my drinking water for a week, and on Saturday night, after everyone was asleep, I washed the crud and smell off my body, then tiptoed naked to the Viking's bunk and crawled in. I snuggled up against his warm, clean body. He rolled over toward me, looked right into my eyes and reached up with his hand to brush the hair away from my eyes.

Then all hell broke loose! Men on deck were yelling Ahoy! and Avast! all over the place, screaming something about a Great White Whale and telling Captain Chris to come look because they thought it might be the one they call The Dick! Everybody around us got up and ran up on deck to see the whale. I didn't move. I didn't want to go anywhere. I guess the Viking didn't either because he didn't move. Just when I was about to reach out and touch him, somebody started banging on the side of the bunk with a stick or something! Shit! *Mierda!*

I opened my eyes. It was the fucking *policía!*

"*Putas! Amaricados!*" *policía* was shouting!

The waves were throbbing against the side of the ship.

I tried to explain to the cop how we'd gotten drunk and passed out here and because there were four of us and only two good bunks we had to double up.

Policía wanted to know, "*Que cuatro?*" What four?

He was right. MikenToby weren't there. They must have gotten up early and gone back to the *pensión*. Fuck!

My left arm was throbbing because I had slept on it all night and cut off the circulation.

Günter was still asleep.

I tried to explain to the cop what had happened, but my Spanish just wasn't coming through the hangover.

My head was throbbing. I decided that dry red wine and sangría were not meant to be consumed together in vat quantities.

Günter woke up. He couldn't figure out what was going on. Hell, he didn't know where we were.

The cop decided to let us go.

Up until that moment, I had not tried to move. As I swung my legs off the bunk, sharp agonizing pain shot out from my groin in every possible direction! Stone aches!

My balls were throbbing because I had just had a six-hour erection without being able to do anything about it! My knees buckled when my feet touched the floor. Günter had to help me off the ship.

The *policía* shouted something about if we ever showed our *maricón* asses around that harbor again he was going to see to it that we got what we were looking for . . . with a mast! And that we were going to hell for desecrating their shrine to the beloved Columbus!

We went to breakfast.

I'll rephrase that. We went to a café. Günter had breakfast. I sipped on the strongest cup of coffee ever made on the face of this planet.

"What happened?" he asked.

"We got our fag asses busted on a national shrine."

"What?"

"He thought we were fucking under Columbus' nose."

"Asshole."

"Exactly." I was sitting on the very front edge of the bench with my legs spread as far apart as I could get them, trying to give my nuts all the room they seemed to be demanding. It didn't help. I winced in pain.

"What's the matter?" he asked.

"Oh nothing . . . just a . . . little . . . ah . . . pain . . . in my . . . uh . . . back," I lied.

"Did you sleep wrong?"

"You can say that again."

We sat silently for a few moments. He ate. I dug out a chunk of my coffee with a spoon and sucked on it.

"My head hurts," Günter said.

"Yeah, mine too."

More silence, longer this time.

"Are you sleeping with that guy William?" I asked. It had to be the hangover talking; I've made an art out of avoiding such confrontations.

"That is none of your fucking business," he said.

My aren't we testy this morning. Speaking of which, I wonder if his testes hurt as much as mine do. Probably not. He probably didn't even get a hard-on last night. (My "adventure at the crotch" was so brief I didn't even have time to identify specific parts of his anatomy.)

"Sorry," I said.

"Uh," he grunted.

"It's just that it's very difficult for me to understand how you can fuck around with him and think it's all right because he's rich, but you won't have sex with me," I blurted out before I had time to visualize how he was probably going to beat the shit out of me if I didn't shut up.

"Look *Scheisskopf*, I'm no queer," he said.

"I didn't say you were. I just want to know why you won't . . ."

"If you want to get fucked, go out and wiggle your ass at one of the horny sailors. There are hundreds of them out there and I hope they fuck your brains out!"

He stood up and walked toward the door.

"Günter, wait . . ."

"*Arschficker*," he said and was gone.

Oh great. Couldn't keep your mouth shut, could you stupid? Had to nag him about it. Couldn't give him a little time and room. No, not you. He didn't throw you out of that bunk last night, remember asshole?

I went for a walk, hoping to clear some of the confusion in my head and some, if not all, of the pain in my groin. I was wondering if it could possibly hurt like that all day. It could.

There's a vulgar expression in Spanish that goes: ¡*Me cago en los veinticuatro cojones de los apóstoles de Jesús*! which loosely translates as "Goddamn it all to hell!" but literally translates "I take a shit on the twenty-four testicles of the apostles of Jesus!" That is precisely the way I felt at that moment.

I started berating myself again as I walked the narrow cobblestone streets of the harbor district: You dumb shit! You dumb shit. What is the matter with you? Last night, the whole time you were lying there in his arms . . . before you passed out . . . you couldn't stop going

on about how life couldn't be better, how you couldn't ask for anything more than that. I know. It really did feel terrific. For the first
time in my entire existence, I felt safe, warm . . . and loved. Now I'm
alone again. Unsafe. Unwarm. Unloved.

I felt like I was in a giant pit and every time I tried to climb out,
the walls would crumble and I'd fall back down to the bottom. Like
a doodlebug trapping ants, I thought. Doodlebugs are the babies of
ant lions. The mama lion digs an almost perfect cone in the sand and
lays her egg at the base of it. Then an ant comes walking along and
falls down into the cone. The walls are so smooth that the ant just
keeps falling back down to the bottom until he dies. Then the little
larva, called a doodlebug, eats it. I used to sit for hours watching that
drama played out over and over again, moving from one cone to the
next, sometimes rooting for the ant as he screamed and tried to claw
his way out, but usually for the doodlebug.

I wondered if Günter went back to William's house.

I walked by a merchant who was flattening octopi out in the sun.
Maybe they were squids; it's hard to tell them apart when they're flat-
tened out like that. There was a scroungy old alley cat poised in the
doorway, hoping the merchant would turn his back for a minute.

I almost fucked a cat once. It was the Mother's cat, Bootsie. It was
probably around third or fourth grade and I was home alone one Saturday afternoon watching television. As was always my custom in those
early years, I got naked the minute she went out the door. So I was
streched out on the floor on my back, half-watching the TV and half-
watching my little pecker sticking straight up in the air when Bootsie
jumped up on my belly. I started to push her off, but changed my
mind when I noticed she was staring at It. She sniffed It. It twitched.
Suddenly I got scared. What if she thought It was a mouse and bit
It? I froze. She licked It. It twitched again. She ran out her little cat
door on the service porch before I could catch her.

I wondered if I would ever see Günter again.

I stood for the longest time in front of a bakery, just staring at the
pastries through the window. I counted over twenty layers of stuff in
this one yellow rectangle one. Another one looked like it had four

different jams in it. They had the biggest coconut macaroons I'd ever seen anywhere. And down in the front, right by the window, they had these funny little loaves of bread that were small and round with a little point right in the middle on the top. They looked like . . .

TITS!!! I forgot the women's tits! How thoughtless of me! I just don't notice them as much as I used to but I know a lot of people do like them. So let's see, who have you met so far?

Stacey. Stacey looked like a little boy, but I assume she had some, even though they didn't stick out or anything. Knowing her, they were probably cute.

Dierdre had Ivy League breasts. They all had to be uniform. By all I mean all the breasts in the school. Girl preppies don't grow their own. At thirteen, they go to Pert Breast Cloning Centers for installation and maintenance instructions. A certificate is forwarded to the school of their choice. You've probably heard how difficult it is to get into some of those eastern schools. Now you know why.

María. María was a Montgomery Ward version of Sophia Loren. I mean that kindly. She was beautiful and sexy, but in a nonglamorous way. An Everyperson.

The Mother. I don't remember. I mean, now she's dowdy and it's all sort of lumped together, but I don't have a human image of her from my youth.

I suppose we'd better do the men, too.

Günter was simply Apollo. Period.

Toby was lumpy like the Mother.

Mike had swimmer's pecs. Nice.

Biff wan't bad either . . . for a jerk.

Wally's you know about already—nauseating and covered with wallpaper stains.

Is that everybody? Me? I don't have a chest. Just think of nipples on an ironing board and you've got it.

I remember as a kid we didn't pay much attention to our nipples. Maybe they don't get erogenous until you reach full manhood, whatever that is. "About as good as teats on a boar," we kids used to say and then giggle. I remember some of the bigger jerks around school would grab a nipple and squeeze so hard that it would hurt for three days, but I don't remember ever going into absolute ecstasy from someone running their tongue around it and biting it ever-so-gently until it got hard and nibbling and licking at the gypsy hairs surrounding it, which get wet and matted from the . . . STOP THAT!!! Geez-Us!

I wondered if I did see Günter again, if things could ever be the way they were before I shot my mouth off.

I discovered that my subconscious had led me back to the *pensión*, and I started thinking how lucky I was to have met Stacey. I was really going to need her now. I remembered how like magic her name sounded when she first said it back on the pier that day. She was magic. I felt better just thinking about her.

I wondered if I went out on the plazas later that night, maybe I'd find Günter and apologize to him and tell him we could just be friends if that's what he wanted and tell him I'd never question him about his . . . about everything and . . .

I was standing inside the *pensión*. Stacked all over the entryway was luggage! Their luggage! Stacey's luggage! MikenToby's luggage! Ken and Barbiedoll's luggage! Wally's luggage! And they were standing around their luggage!

"What's the meaning of this?!! Where were you two this morning?! Are you all right, Stacey?"

She nodded.

Toby answered, "Stacey came back to get us early this morning and you two looked like you didn't want to be disturbed, so we just left you."

"In what way did we look like we didn't want to be disturbed?" I demanded to know. I wasn't challenging him, I was dying of curiosity.

"Peaceful slumber," Mike said.

Damn.

"What is all this? Where are you going? Why didn't you tell me?" I ranted some more.

"Luggage."

"Africa."

"We just found out," I think Wally said. I'd never heard his voice before. He was walking kind of funny, but he didn't seem to have any

cuts or bruises on him. I was glad of that. I would hate to think I
was responsible for. . . .

"AFRICA?!" Talk about your betrayals!

"Yeah, Casablanca," someone said.

"You can't go to Africa," I gasped.

"We have to go; it's our job," Stacey said. She knew it was really
her I was talking about.

"I won't let you!" I blocked the door dramatically. Sometimes I can
be a real jerk.

"You're being a jerk," Stacey said insightfully.

"Some magic you turned out to be!" I shouted.

"What are you talking about?" she asked.

"Magic. The magic of companionship. The magic of laughter. The
magic of . . . oh shit! Whatayou care!"

"You're sick," she said.

"And you're a cunt with a capital *K*!" I said, hating myself immediately. My knees got weak. I sat down on one of the larger suitcases
and the pain from my balls reached from my toes to my tear ducks.
I was crying.

"How dare you call me that! You spend the whole night with that
blond stud you've been drooling over all week and you have the nerve
to call me a cunt?! You, you faggot!!"

"Jealous?" I accused.

"Stacey!" Mike stepped in.

I sobbed.

"Oh Tad, I'm sorry," Stacey said, starting to cry with me and throwing her arms around me. I didn't tell her the real reason I was crying.
I wasn't sure what the real reason was, actually.

"I wish you wouldn't use that word, Stacey," Mike said.

"She can use any words she wants. He shouldn't have called her that!"
Toby joined in.

"People shouldn't call other people faggot, faggot" Mike shouted.

"Isn't that the pot calling the kettle black?" Toby asked.

"Well, you should know about pots, Moby Dick!"

"Guys, please." I said, still weeping.

"*Toby* Dick if you don't mind!" Toby added.

"Hey, I had a dream about that last night," I said.

"Shut up, Tad!" Toby Dick said.

Moby Dick caused me to flunk freshman English. The first day of class, I made the mistake of asking if the name *Moby Dick* meant anything and was requested to leave the lecture hall for making the girls blush and the boys laugh. Then, while the rest of the class was trying to identify all of Melville's metaphors, and there seem to be thousands, I was researching the name. I was never able to discover the origin of the name and, as I said, I flunked the class, but I did find out that *dick* is a very popular word:

Besides being the diminutive of Richard, it also is a hard cheese, a plain pudding (or if pudding with treacle sauce, then treacle dick) and is used to mean everyman as in Tom, Dick and Harry. A spotted dick is a current or raisin pudding. There's a leather apron called a dick. A riding whip – a gold-headed dick if it is so ornamented. A dick-a-dilver is a periwinkle. A dick-a-Tuesday is a will-o'-the-wisp. A dick-ass is a jackass. There's a hedge sparrow called a dickdunno. Dick is an abbreviation for the word dictionary. Dick means a ditch or its bank or dike. To take one's dick means to make a declaration. To be up to dick means that something is up to the standard. In America, dick is used to mean detective. A test for scarlet fever is known as the Dick test, named for its developers – a pair of Dicks who were American physicians. Dick also means penis (often considered vulgar).

"Real smart cocksucker, aren't you?" Mike said. They were still going at each other! The others had taken the luggage out to Wally's car.

"I would be if I could get past your smelly foreskin!" Toby retorted.

"My foreskin does not smell!" Mike assured everyone.

"It's like I used to tell my wife: If you want it licked, honey, you're going to have to start keeping it clean!"

"Toby!" Stacey scolded.

I wanted to step in and try to stop them but I was afraid to!

"What *wife*! A female wife?" Mike asked. "You never said anything about a wife. Two years we've been together and wife never came up."

"I told you I used to do it with girls," Toby said.

"You told me girls, yes . . . and I forgave you. You never told WIFE!"

"If you're going to get hysterical, I'm not going to tell you about it," Toby said.

"I don't want you to tell me about it!"

"Good, because I'm not going to!" Toby said.

"Good," Mike said, refusing to cry.

Silence. Maybe it's over. No.

"How long were you married, asshole," Mike asked. He sounded so hurt. And vulnerable.

"I wasn't," Toby said.

"What's that supposed to mean?" We all wanted to know, but Mike was the one to ask.

"I wasn't married. I made it up," Toby said.

"What?" That was Stacey and me.

"I made it up. I was never married. Never even came close."

"What a shit!" we all thought, but Mike was the one to say it out loud.

"All's fair in love and bitch fights, as they say," Toby jested. No one laughed.

"You're an asshole! A rotten, no-good, underhanded asshole!" Mike screamed, but you could see that he was relieved.

"Your father wears espadrilles!" Toby said.

"What?"

"I think I resent that," I said.

"You're supposed to say, 'Your mother wears combat boots!' " Stacey instructed.

That was about where I started to giggle.

"His mother does wear combat boots . . . it wouldn't be an insult," Toby said, trying to suppress his giggles.

"They are not combat boots," Mike insisted. "They're construction boots! She's a goddamn contractor! You want her to wear high heels on the job for chrissake?!" He was laughing so hard at that point, he barely got the last sentence out.

Stacey and I fell off the suitcase we were sitting on. I thought I was going to pass out from the pain. MikenToby helped me off the floor before they gave each other a big kiss and hug to make up.

I walked with them out to the car.

Mike and I shook hands. Toby gave me a hug and a kiss which earned him a glare from Mike. I still hadn't figured out the hostility I was feeling from him. I wondered if he thought I had been coming on to him or if he thought Toby had been coming on to me. I wondered if I was going to survive without these people.

MikenToby got into the back seat of the car. Wally and Mr. and Mrs. Wonderful were already in the front seat.

Stacey and I just stared at each other.

"You know how I hate good-byes," she said.

"Yeah."

"Look, we'll be at the Hotel Claire, right next to the Moulin Rouge . . ."

There's that damn Red Mill again.

". . . in Casablanca. You do whatever you have to do to get down there and we'll work it out from there. Okay?" She took a tear from my left eye.

"Okay."

"Bring Günter if you can. I mean that."

"Sure." My throat was so damned tight I couldn't do complicated words.

She pulled me aside, out of earshot of the others.

"He's not your type," she said.

"He's not yours either."

"Maybe so, but I'm not the one pursuing him."

"I'm not pursuing him," I insisted. "Am I?"

"You seem to be. And that's okay—it's your life. But what happens if you catch him? What happens if you two do get together?"

"We'll live happily every after?" I wondered.

"Maybe."

"All my life I've been looking for someone to love, someone who'd love me back. Is that so bad?"

"No, but the part about loving back is . . ."

"Impossible."

"Not impossible, damn it, but it is the more difficult of the two . . . as I'm sure you know."

"Boy do I." Boy did I.

"We can't always plan everything out; goals are great to have, but we don't always set the right goals for ourselves; sometimes things just happen, if we let them. Take me, for example. I . . ."

"Is this going to be another food story?" I asked.

"No! It's a *me* story. I came to Europe thinking all I wanted—all I needed—was to absorb the atmosphere: The architecture, the music, the art, the landscape, the history. But you know what I found? I found that what I needed was people. I needed to be closer to people. And, as screwed up as our little family is, they've come to mean a lot to me. More than I ever thought was possible for me. Even Dierdre and Biffff. Forget Wally. And Mike and Toby are like brothers to me—we really love each other. I think we all do. And hell, a few weeks ago, I thought I'd found it all. Then I found you. You are so special, Tadpole. You're the specialest of all. I don't ever want to lose you. I care about you. I *worry* about you! I want you to make all your dreams come true—especially Günter, if you're sure he's what you really want. And I'll be the happiest of them all if everything works out right. I really will! But I'll also be around if it doesn't. And you damn well better come running to me first, you asshole."

"Jesus, Trish, don't go!"

You've heard of the floodgates opening? Well, the dam broke on that one. I started bawling around "specialest" and she let loose on "worry." Together we ended Spain's worst drought of the century.

We hugged. Then we kissed. Then we hugged again.

"Seeya Tadpole."

"Seeya Trish."

They drove away.

I went up to my room, locked the door, closed the blinds, undressed, went to bed and cried myself to sleep.

6. Morocco Bound!

The camel was eating my hair! There is nothing I hate more than having a fucking camel eat my hair! Except maybe camels themselves. They spit. A lot. They are easily one of the top two disgusting animals on this earth. The other being baboons with red, bulbous asses, out of which they pick shit and throw it at unsuspecting zoo visitors whilst farting selections from Sousa marches.

Anyway, in my dream, I was leading this camel across the desert with my master perched up on the back on one of those funny camel saddles. He was a one-humper. The camel, not my master. My master had long, dark hair and dark eyes and a dark beard. He had a desert tan and always wore a white burnous. He was awe inspiring . . . almost godlike.

We went up on this high dune in the hope of finding an oasis where we could camp for the night. I was standing there in front of the camel, looking around for trees or water or anything! when I felt this wet glob hit the back of my neck. I figured the goddamn camel was spitting again, so I turned around to slap the ugly fucker on the lips. What I discovered was that it wasn't the camel at all! It was my master, deep in the throes of self-abuse! On top of a camel? In broad daylight? I prostrated myself. Not out of worship or anything like that, although that's the way I felt about him, but because a slave is not allowed to look upon his master's erect penis . . . unless specifically invited to do so. Especially when he is masturbating! And masters do that . . . at least mine does . . . often! Seems like I'm always having to prostrate myself.

My master and I found an oasis. I put up the tent and prepared dinner. After we ate, the master bathed. I watched him disrobe. He wasn't erect, so it was all right. It probably wasn't all right for me to be drooling, but he didn't see that. He walked out on the glimmering, moonlit pool and then lowered himself down into the water. Let me tell you: I was impressed!

After his bath, he walked naked to the tent, his wet, olive skin glistening in the moonlight. I had my own little tent sticking out the front of my burnous. He looked at it. Masters are allowed to look at a slave's erection. Hell, anybody can look at a slave's erection. He went into the tent and I curled up in my usual place in the sand just outside the flap.

I made a little hole in the sand with my fist and rolled over onto it. Slaves aren't allowed to masturbate. You can get "beheaded" for it. I'd just got to going good on it when my master called out. Shit! He ordered me to take a bath and then come into the tent. Hotdiggidy! I was out of my dirty old robe and into the water in two seconds flat. Boy, that water felt good. It had been weeks since my last bath. The crud was coming off of me in cakes, like mud. I languished in the tub, as I'd heard people who have tubs often do. It means you stay in the water so long that you get weak. I stayed in the water so long I got yelled at.

The master was getting impatient. I don't know what I thought I was doing: I wanted to get in that tent just as much as he wanted me to. I ran to the tent, naked in breathless anticipation of a night of love-making. I threw open the flap with a flourish — my penis proudly saluting my master. I could've shit! There must've been a hundred people in that tent! All in their formal robes! The sonofabitch was having a cocktail party! And he wanted me to serve the fucking hors d'oeuvres!

I was mortified! I was incensed! I was limp.

Someone was knocking at the flap.

It was Günter.

William had thrown Günter's ass out into the street and I guess he thought he could bring it to me. Of course he could. I invited him in.

"What happened?" I asked.

"Kaiser Wilhelm threw me out!" he said.

"That's terrible," I said. Serves you right, you prick-teasing bastard, I thought.

"I am sorry for what I said to you," he apologized.

"That's okay. Forget it."

"It is okay for us to be friends now?"

"Yeah, sure," I mumbled. I was sure I wasn't deluding myself about him. He was a user and he was about to use me. What could I do? I wanted him to.

"Even if I don't want to make love with you?"

"Yeah . . . even if." Rub it in, asshole.

"I do not have a place to live now," he said.

"What about your friend, Pamela?" I asked.

"How do you know about Pamela?"

"You mentioned her that night on the hill."

"Oh."

I felt a little guilty about enjoying his predicament, but no so guilty that I couldn't push a little.

"Won't she help you?"

"She went to Amsterdam."

"That's a shame. Why did William throw you out, anyway?" I asked.

"He said I should not stay away all night from his house and I told him he did not own me and that I would go anywhere I wanted, when I wanted. So he said I should do that, now! And I did. I will have to go back up there to get my clothes. I was so angry I forgot to take them with me."

"If he'll let you in to get them."

"He will have to let me in."

"Maybe you're better off without him," I said. My mind was running a mile a minute. I was sure he was a hustler. He had made it abundantly clear he didn't want to be my lover. I didn't have enough money to buy him. If I didn't put him out of my life altogether, my frustration level was going to reach an all-time high.

"You may be right, but I must find somewhere to live," he said.

"It helps." I was stalling.

"May I stay here with you?" he asked, looking me straight in the eyes.

"No." Shockwaves! I actually said No!

"Why not?" he asked.

"They charge by the person here. You would have to pay." That wasn't what I meant, but it was true.

"Oh. What about your friends? Can they help?"

He's got a fucking lot of nerve, I thought. Go find your own friends to use and leave mine out of it.

"They went to Casablanca," I said.

"Um," he muttered . . . then, "you want to go?"

"Go where?"

"To Casablanca to see your friends."

"You want to go to Morocco?"

"Yes."

"With me?"

"Yes."

"Okay." I didn't believe I had said that. It's hard to combat your own stupidity.

"*Gut!*" There's that native tongue of his I told you I wanted to lapse into.

"When?" I asked.

"Now."

"Now?"

"*Ja!* You get ready while I go back to William's house to get my clothes. I will return in maybe an hour."

I grunted something.

He ran out the door. I sat on the edge of the bed wondering if I had totally lost my mind. The answer was yes. I jumped up, raced out the door and downstairs to tell *La Familia del pensión de las Flores*.

I was going to Africa! Sonofabitch!!

Pensión de las Flores
322 Las Ramblas
Barcelona, España

Hi Mom!

I guess you must know by now that I didn't go to Hawaii with Grant and Jeanie. And, as you can see, I went east instead of west. I'm sorry if I caused you any worry.

I'm not exactly sure what happened. We were all set to go, packed and everything, but the last week before we were supposed to leave got so weird that I just couldn't go with them. They had been a little standoffish all week, maybe having second thoughts about my going along on their vacation. Then on Saturday night, the three of us went out to dinner and I guess we had too much to drink because things started getting nasty around dessert. (No, I am not drinking too much! Just enough! Ha Ha.) Anyway, they were arguing with each other, but it was very obvious it was me they were really upset with. So I invited myself into the fight and within an hour nobody was speaking to anyone else. It was a very quiet and very long ride back to their house.

I went straight to my room and they to theirs. I don't know if they made up or not, because I got up early the next morning, grabbed my bags and headed for the airport and New York City. It was a little difficult in Manhattan with only my Hawaii clothes, but I didn't stay that long anyway. The clothes are fine in Barcelona. It's nice and warm here.

I guess it was a mistake to try and share a house with them. I think people stay friends longer if they don't have to see each other every day. I probably would've moved out of there even if the big blow-up hadn't happened that night. (No, I could not have come to stay with you! We tried that, remember! Besides, we want to stay friends, don't we? See above.)

I hope Ruth from the bank hasn't been bothering you. I'm sorry if she has. I always thought it was a mistake to give her your number. In fact, I wouldn't have given it to her if you hadn't insisted. Anyway, the next time you talk to her (why do I suspect you two talk every day?), tell her that I'm sorry to have left without giving proper notice and that I won't be back. I think they owe me three weeks pay (including the vacation pay). Would you see if she'll give the check to you? You can send it to me here. I may be doing some traveling, but they'll forward it to me or I can come back and pick it up.

I'm sorry to put you to so much trouble. I promise when I get back (No, I don't know when that will be), I'll make it up to you somehow.

I'll write to them later, but if you go over to Grant and Jeanie's (make that "when"), in the closet in my room, there's . . .

A knock at the door.

"*Venga!*"

"*Lo siento mucho, señor, pero yo tengo que limpiar su cuarto,*" the cute little señor junior said.

Real cute. About fourteen or fifteen at the most. Long black hair. Lean boyish muscles. His first mustache just attaining visibility. Wearing absolutely nothing but cutoffs!

"*Está bien,*" I stammered and motioned for him to go ahead with his cleaning.

I tried to get back to my work, the letter, but my mind was blank. Well not blank exactly, but definitely nothing I could write to the Mother.

Here's a blow-by-blow description of what followed.

If only he were wearing some clothes, I thought. It's a lot easier to ignore it if you can't see it all.

My god! he's playing with himself! He's down on his hand and knees scrubbing the tile and touching it about every other scrub!

I'm leaving town and this little fucker decides to get horny!

Don't do it, Tad! They probably have very long prison sentences here for this sort of thing. C'mon, settle down! You've never been interested in chicken! Don't start now!

If he keeps playing with it like that, it's going to come sneaking out of those cutoffs. Don't look!

His father probably told him the cocksucker up in room *seis* was leaving town and the kid thought he'd better get his in before I shoved off.

What am I worrying about? I'm in love with Günter and when I'm in love I don't even think about sex with other people. Well, maybe I think about it a little, but I don't do anything about it. Don't really want to . . . even when it's staring me in the face like this, defying gravity and my will power!

Oh shit! There it is! Put that thing away!

I swear I didn't mean to be unfaithful. Honest. It's just that he . . . uh . . . and I . . . . this is very difficult . . . oh shit! He whipped it out and I dove for it! There, it's said! A person's only human after all. Think of it as a gift for my hosts. When you stay in someone's home, you're supposed to give them a little something when you leave. Junior was one of my hosts. ("Thank you for having me as a guest in your home. Here's a little blow job as a token of my appreciation!") And remember how frustrated I was after sleeping in you-know-whose arms all night on the Santa Maria—platonically! I'm sorry! I couldn't help myself! I'm weak! I know it! Sob!

The little señor junior pulled his shorts back up and left with his pail and brush and a noticeable smirk on his face. I wondered if he had said good-bye this overtly to MikenToby before they left for Casablanca.

Is chicken still chicken when the other one is chicken, too? Rather than some old rooster? Like my first *LIVE* lover, the boy who moved next door the day before my eleventh birthday. Best birthday I ever had.

Charley was twelve and had that tousled, white-blond hair they call towhead. He was a little bigger than I was and, as it turned out, twice as horny.

My party was on Sunday afternoon and Charley and his family moved in on Saturday. I spent the whole day just watching them carry things into the house from the truck and their station wagon.

I watched the boy the closest though, because I wondered what he was like. There were no boys my age in our neighborhood and I hated everyone at my school and I was hoping this boy would turn out to be someone I could play with. I mean stuff like catch and marbles and other boy stuff. I didn't know yet that other people played with their peepees and I couldn't have guessed in a million years that people did it together! To each other!

The Mother sent me to bed early that night with the old standby about how I was going to have a big day tomorrow. If she only knew! I turned off my light and sat at my window to stare at the house next door. They were still running around putting things away. There was the usual mom and dad and the boy, but all of a sudden there was a baby, too. I hadn't seen that earlier. I figured some relative had taken care of it during the day while they were moving and then dropped it off after dinner.

They finally got finished or just too tired to do anymore and they all went to bed.

The mom wore a robe and a nightgown underneath it. The dad had on pajamas. They slept in the same bed. She got in on one side and he got in on the other, but they turned the light off right away so I didn't learn anything from them.

The boy was a whole other story! He didn't turn off his lights or close his drapes. I swear he got naked in less than ten seconds. My record is fifteen seconds. His peepee was sticking straight out. It gave me a funny feeling like when I used to imagine this whole long row of boys, a hundred of them maybe, lined up all around this huge swimming pool with their little peckers sticking straight out like that and perfectly lined up, too.

Anyway, the boy stood up on his bed and kept turning to one side and then the other. I couldn't figure out what the hell he was doing until I saw the mirror on top of his dresser. Interesting! I made a mental note to ask the Mother for a mirror for my room. He dropped to his knees, arched his back way back and went at it!

So did I!

When I got to know him better, I asked him if he had left his lights on and his drapes open on purpose that night . . . . did he know I was watching? He did.

Anyway, I ran over there right after breakfast the next morning and invited him to my birthday party.

"But you hate meeting new children," the Mother said to me.

"I've gotta get over that sometime," I told her.

Most of the party was awful. Since I had refused to invite any of the shitheads from my school, the Mother had blackmailed or bribed her friends into bringing their brats to my party and most of them were younger, so they didn't understand any of the games. Finally, the mothers all went into the kitchen to yak and left us kids to ourselves after getting us started on a game of hide-and-seek.

Charley and I wound up in my closet playing show-and-tell. And touch. I remember how strange it felt touching someone else's and having someone else touch mine. We did it for hours.

The Mother was furious! Everyone had gone home and it took her a half-hour to find us. Didn't you hear me calling you? No. We did, though. Fortunately. We barely got our shorts pulled back up before she flung the closet door open!

I went back to my letter:

Sorry for the interruption, Mom, but the maid had to clean my room.

Anyway, when you go over to Grant and Jeanie's, please get my box of tax stuff out of my closet. I'm going to need it sometime next spring wherever I am.

I've met some really nice young people over here. I'm hoping some of them will become permanent friends.

And—brace yourself—I've been trying my hand at writing Poetry! I know the poems are not very good yet, but I am learning and I'm having a lot of fun writing them. It's an interesting process my mind goes through when I sit down, pen in hand, to compose one. Right now I'm heavily influenced by Arthur Rimbaud (that's Ramboh if you're not familiar with him) who was a nineteenth-century French poet. I hope eventually to grow into my own, but in the meantime I don't mind too much because I find his imagery fascinating. I am enclosing one poem I wrote a couple of weeks ago. It's called "Afrika."

I'll write again soon. I promise! As I said, you can write to me here at this address and I'll get it sooner or later.

I am sorry for all this. I know how it must have upset you when I disappeared like that. There was nothing else I could've done.

Love to all,
Tad

AFRIKA

The hot sirocco wind dries
   the sweat from my naked loins.
My lover, Afrika, embraces me.

He is the beautiful Hermaphroditus,
      so glorious in his ambivalence.
The woman I am. The man I am.

He clutches me to his pulsating breast,
      the sand burning my tender flesh.
I surrender to his deadly passion.

His million fingers caress my body,
      covering me with his fevered warmth.
He engulfs my groin, suffocates my soul.

He mounts me—intent on his cruel rape—
      his crushing weight upon my chest.
He devours me as we begin our loving thrust.

My sweet Hermaphroditus! My sweet Afrika!
      deliver me unto my destiny!
Enter me that we may become one.

The burning grains of his love fill my insides,
      scorching my throat, searing my bowels.
Afrika is love! Afrika is me! I am Afrika!

                              —Tad Prescott

I knew I'd wind up apologizing to her later for that poem, but I couldn't resist the temptation. Mothers need a jolt now and then, particularly mothers who thrive on aggravation. It keeps them young.

I packed my suitcases and I was stuffing the last pair of socks in a corner when Günter returned.

"Any trouble?" I asked.

"No. He even gave me some money so we could take the train."

"You're kidding?"

"No."

"Maybe he's not such a bad guy after all," I said. I was beginning to wonder how it is that some people learn how to get things out of other people and the rest of us don't.

"What are all these for?" he asked.

"All what?"

"These, uh, suitcases."

"They're for the trip. What else?"

"You cannot take all these on a third-class train, and we may have to hitch the last part of the trip."

All he had was a backpack.

"It'll be all right. I'll take care of them." I've never understood why I've always insisted on doing things my own way, even when I know the other person is right.

"It is your problem then," he said.

"I said it would be!"

He took two sweaters out of his pack. He had stopped on his way back to the *pensión* to buy them for us. They were the same style and knit, but different colors. He bought a black one for himself. Mine was red. I guess he thought my wardrobe needed a splash of color. He looked like Don Juan in his. I looked like Don Knotts.

I stopped downstairs on our way out to say good-bye to *la familia*. The señor shook my hand and gave Günter a funny look. The señora gave me a *buena suerta* hug and kiss and gave Günter a funny look. The assorted señoritas and señor juniors sort of nodded and/or grunted, looking at their feet. My little señor junior from earlier that day was conspicuously absent. The señora said he had gone to church, bless his little heart, and that she would tell him I said good-bye.

Günter helped me carry my luggage to the train station.

7. Bobadilla, Cha Cha Cha!

"Once upon a time in a place very far away from here, in a big lily pond in your great Aunt Emma's backyard, there lived a Daddy Frog and a Mommy Frog and eight little-bitty Tadpoles.

"Now, the Daddy Frog was a great big bull frog and he had a great big voice, 'CROAK CROAK.' The Mommy Frog was a medium-size frog with a much smaller voice, 'croak croak.' But the eight little-bitty Tadpoles didn't make any noise at all because they weren't even frogs yet.

"Well, there was this one Tadpole; he was the smallest of all the little-bitty Tadpoles—sort of the runt of the litter you could say. Anyway, he was always being a bad little boy and the Mommy Frog was always having to scold him and the Daddy Frog was always having to spank him because he just wouldn't mind them.

"He swam in all the places he was told not to swim. He would stick his tiny little nose out of the water when the mean old birds were by the pond, which he had been told a thousand times not to do. He nipped his little brothers and sisters on their little tails, which everyone knows could cause them to lose their tails too soon . . . and then they would never be able to become frogs! Ever! His daddy spanked him for biting his brothers' and sisters' tails and his mommy told him that if he ever bit their tails again she was going to send him off to the orphanage.

"Well, do you know what that naughty little Tadpole did? I'll tell you what that bad little boy did. He started nipping at his own little tail! His mommy was beside herself. She got so upset she started to cry and she pleaded with him not to play with his little tail. She told him, again and again, how he would not be able to become a frog . . . ever . . . because 'if you don't stop playing with it, it will fall off!'

"Well, that bad little Tadpole didn't listen to his mother and he just kept right on nipping at his own little tail and, sure enough, just like his mommy had warned him, it did fall off and he never got to be a frog!"

The Mother told me that cute little story when I was eight years old. I didn't get it.

Then she caught me playing with my peepee under the kitchen sink one day when I thought she was gone. She said, "What did I tell you about the little Tadpole who kept playing with himself?"

Then I got it. Oh shit!

Then I stopped playing with it.

We had a wet toilet seat for two weeks. I wasn't about to touch that thing . . . not even to aim!

But then Teddy Bear Sam got so lonely that I decided to risk it. (Decided hell, I lost control and raped the poor little bastard!) So what if I never got to be a frog!

Then I remembered she had said something about the Tadpole losing his tail too soon. Too soon?!! That meant it was going to fall off anyway! Goddamn! I redoubled by efforts, vowing to get as much out of it as I could before the damn thing fell off!

It still hasn't fallen off after all these years, but I've kept my vow just in case.

I was the only one awake in our crowded little compartment. I was running out of self-amusements and with seven other people in there I thought I shouldn't masturbate. I would've like to, though. We were jammed in there so tight that Günter's elbow was in my crotch. Those damn benches were only four normal butts wide and at least two of the butts on our bench weren't normal.

Yes, I said bench. Spanish third-class trains are a phenomenon unto themselves. Unique. The wooden bench we had was, as I said, about four butts wide, but it was only ten or twelve inches deep, so I had to keep pushing myself back against the wall behind me to keep from sliding off. And the bench opposite was so close that my knees were bumping the person's knees in front of me, a rather large Chilean woman whose taste for garlic had been the cause of the drunken party earlier that night.

I remember having freaked out slightly when I first saw our compartment. We'd caught the midnight train out of Barcelona, and I had pretty much assumed there wouldn't be anybody else on the train at that time of night. Günter led us down the center walkway in search of our assigned compartment. He stopped in front of one that already had six people in it! I argued that he had to be mistaken – surely these compartments are limited to four people and this one already had six! Not so. There were four little ticket brackets above the bench on each side . . . and that makes eight total. We squeezed in. Günter's backpack easily swung up onto the luggage rack and out of the way. My suitcases, on the other hand, were heavy and bulky and awkward and generally impossible to stow. Everyone stared at me.

Besides the Chilean woman who ate garlic, our traveling companions included a French student on holiday, a Spanish soldier, a married couple going to the wife's mother's funeral in one of the mountain villages and a very old man who never said a word. He had his dog with him.

Without thinking, I pulled out my Marlboros, lit one and gave one to Günter. Suddenly the whole damn compartment was astir with "Yes, thank you," "*Oui s'il vous plait*" and "*Sí gracias.*" Seems as though one doesn't partake of anything unless you intend to share it with all. That turned out to our benefit, though. We had forgotten to bring food. They don't have club cars. But there was enough food for an army in the baskets our roommates brought with them. Cheese, bread, fruit, some kind of beef stick (I think) and garlic. We all passed on the garlic. The woman peeled a clove for herself and then bit into it, nibbling like a rabbit and running her tongue around the outside of her mouth, apparently checking for any misplaced morsels. Everything tasted like garlic after that. Even the apple. Someone suggested that wine would clear our taste buds. We all looked to the soldier to see if he was going to forbid the wine drinking on this public conveyance. He smiled and reached into his bag and pulled out a bottle of dry red. He yanked the cork and passed the bottle. We gave him a

mild ovation. Halfway through that bottle, the French student pro-
duced a vintage Bordeaux and got it started around. The Chilean garlic-
eater followed that up with one of the smoothest, full-bodied Caber-
net Sauvignons I'd ever tasted. I just kept passing the cigarettes around,
afraid someone might notice that we hadn't contributed to the feast
and cut us off.

After the singing and dancing (mostly upper body stuff because there
was no room to move your feet), they dropped off one by
one . . . squirming on those hard benches, nestling onto each other's
bodies or the side walls to prevent whiplash from the head falling around
during sleep.

I was finally getting sleepy myself and I began to hallucinate a little
bit in my half-conscious state. I could hear voices coming from the
other compartments. Some were in Spanish, others in French and still
others in languages I didn't recognize. Then very gradually, I started
understanding them all. Perfectly. They weren't changing into English – I
just understood them. They blended with the sounds of the train until
the whole thing mounted to a great chorus! A Beethovanesque Climax!

And sleep.

Dreams ran rampant. Incomprehensible. Garlic dreams of murder
and mutilation. Wine dreams of mayhem and Mother.

I woke in a cold sweat. I had a chill from my damp clothes. My
mouth was dry and there was a large wet spot on Günter's sleeve where
I had apparently drooled on him. I smelled like stale wine and garlic.
Everything smelled like stale wine and garlic. And cigarette butts.

I roused Günter, and we went for a walk up toward the front of
the train. Every compartment in third-class was as cramped and crowded
as ours. Between third and second we ran into some boys with an
urn of coffee. Hot mud. It was perfect. Cleaned the palate like Drano.

Second-class was almost empty and the few who were there had
whole compartments to themselves. Some of the compartments were
totally void of human life. I was most covetous.

They wouldn't let us even walk into the first-class car, so we turned
around and headed back to our meager quarters in the last car of the
train. As we neared our compartment door, I noticed there was a small

landing (terrace? balcony?) outside the door that would've led to the next car if there had been another car on that train. I ran out the door.

Air! I hyperventilated. Günter came out and steadied me before I fell off. I braced myself against the iron railing and tried to suck it all in.

We were in the mountains. Beautiful, green, soft hills surrounded us. Trees zoomed by us on either side of the tracks. We zipped through dozens of short tunnels as we snaked our way through the passes. I was agog. And it was like that all day!

One of the greatest things was seeing everything backwards . . . especially coming out of tunnels that I never saw us going into. It would be like always having to pull out without ever inserting.

I even pissed off the end of the train. That was strange too. Well Günter did it first! (Why is it that whenever boys pee outside, they always have to compete to see who can pee the farthest? I could've won a few of those contests if they would've let me pee off the end of a train. It goes a long, long way.)

For the first time since I'd met Günter, I wasn't in the mood to talk. So, of course, he was.

I missed half of it. I'm looking at wildlife and he's going on about his grandmother. Something about a field and some potatoes. I may be getting him mixed up with a movie I saw once, but like I said I wasn't listening very well.

While I was trying to count tunnels, he told me something about his uncle and a circus clown.

I tried to concentrate, but it wasn't working. I couldn't stay in one place in my head for more than about thirty seconds, so I was missing a lot of good stuff—stuff I could've used on him later.

Like his story about some old person who lived somewhere and who would pay or bribe the little boys to suck them off or touch them or something, but I didn't get whether it was an old man or an old woman or where this all took place or what was paid or exactly what it was that this old person did to or for the little boys. Too bad. That would have been a good one to remember.

The longest span I was able to reach was right after he used the word "hustle" in connection with Pamela, but he was already so far into the story when I tuned in that I couldn't make much sense out of it. I got the part where she was the one who paid for his way to Barcelona in the first place, but I couldn't figure out how they had met or anything. And there was something about Pamela and William knowing each other. Small world, I thought and then tripped out again.

We were passing this magnificent hillside smothered in bright blue flowers! I wanted to roll in them . . . naked.

I got a hard-on.

It reminded me of what we used to call the old school bus boner.

I don't think I ever missed a morning on the school bus without getting an erection. I spent the better part of my academic career holding my notebook over the front of my pants. Most of the guys I knew got school bus boners, but not everyday like I did.

Charley used to whack it with the backside of his hand whenever he caught me with one and he also used to wait for me just outside the bus door—I was always the last one off the bus, hoping it would go down before I had to walk—and then try to grab my notebook out of my clenched hands.

Charley was always doing horny stuff like that. Whenever I'd get aroused in the school library, he'd peak under the table and say, "Got the ol' Tad POLE again, huh?" Just like that. Out loud!

I got even with him, though. I shot all over his mother's brand-new sofa. Scared the shit out of Charley! Our earlier play sessions had always been too short or too mild for me to get off, so he didn't know I could shoot. He hadn't started shooting yet himself . . . and he was almost a year older than I was.

It was a Sunday and his parents were at church. We had been so rambunctious at the breakfast table that morning that his father had refused to go to church if we went along. So we got to stay home, just as we'd planned.

The sofa had just been delivered the day before. It was covered in that plush, velvetlike stuff that stains so easily. All we knew was that it looked really soft and we were dying to see how it felt against our bare skin. We got naked before the car was even out of the driveway.

We guessed right—it felt terrific! We wrestled and bit each other and grabbed everything there was to grab and humped the cracks between the cushions. Then, for the first time in our relationship, we got hold of each other's and really went to town. He got to his still-dry climax first and started making funny little noises. I thought he was getting sick or something so I stopped. I thought he was going to kill me! Then I came! All over the sofa! "Holy shit!" I think is what he said.

After he settled down a little and stopped screaming how I had pissed all over his mother's brand-new couch, I told him how I had heard at school that different guys start shooting at different ages and that he had something really special to look forward to. In the near future, we hoped.

We made some toast and spread apple jelly on it and then dumped it on the sofa over my stuff and then wiped the whole thing up together. Charley was sure he'd get the death penalty, but it was only one week grounded and three month with no allowance. He made me buy his candy bars at school until he got his allowance reinstated.

"Hey!"

"What?" I jumped.

"What are you doing out here?" Günter asked as he stepped back out onto my private train terrace.

"Just thinking."

"What about?"

"A couch."

"A what?"

"Nothing. . .just kidding."

"Do you want something to eat?" he asked, handing me a sandwich and a carton of orange juice.

"Where'd you get the food?" I wondered.

"In the village back there," he said.

"What village?" I asked.

"The little town we just stopped in."

"Oh. . . yeah." Space cadet.

"Are you okay?"

"I'm fine. I was just thinking about the fight I had with my friends before I came to Spain." Obviously it was a lie, but I couldn't tell him the sofa story.

"Were they good friends?" he asked as he sat down on the balcony floor across from me.

"The best. We lived together, the three of us. Grant, Jeanie and me. . . I. We went to the same college together and then just sort of stayed together after that. They were going on vacation to Hawaii just before I left and I was supposed to take care of the house while they were gone. Then something came up about her mother wanting to visit and I wasn't going to be able to stay there and then they talked about canceling their vacation and we all started fighting so I just got the hell out of there and came here."

"How did you do that in one breath?"

"Funny."

"Have you written to them?" he asked.

"Not yet. I don't know what to say." I didn't.

"I know what you mean," he said. "It is like that argument I had with Pamela that I told you about this morning."

What argument with Pamela? What did I miss?

That night, I traded a pack of Marlboros to the French kid for a bottle of his wine and Günter and I made ourselves at home in one of the empty compartments in second-class. The compartments with the padded cushions and the fold-up armrests and the sliding door that actually closes and the window that had been cleaned within the last year. He stretched out on one side and I sat by the window on the other. No one bothered us. Günter dozed off quickly and I was left to try and amuse myself again.

I watched him sleep. Ever watch anyone sleep? People look different when they're asleep. Most people close their eyes when they sleep so that changes their looks somewhat. And they aren't posing, which changes them a whole lot. That's when I noticed that one of Günter's ears was lower than the other. Then he rolled over and I couldn't see his face any longer. He had a small mole behind his right ear.

I think the body is the only personal possession that should be taken seriously. Everything else is too transient to even matter: cars get wrecked or stolen or sold; clothes get worn out or torn or lost or given away or pushed to the back of the closet; houses get ripped off or delapidated or burned down or bulldozed; money . . . disappears. But your body really is yours—and only yours—for as long as you hang around in any one incarnation.

One of the little solitaire games I like to play sometimes is called Body Parts. The idea is to discover some part of your body that you've really never investigated before. You have to get right up on it and learn everything you can about it—every crease, hair, the shape of the bone or bones under the skin, etc. Before that night on the train, I had discovered my knees, elbows, big toes, navel and, of course, my penis. But my penis didn't really count because, long before I ever played that game, I knew it like the back of my hand.

Hand! That's one I hadn't done before.

Very complicated, the hand. I has a lot of bones, tendons, tiny muscles, blood vessels, a million creases, the fingernails and the shit under the fingernails, a dozen little scars and usually a few scratches or cuts that will someday be scars, fingers and finger games, the thumb, palm, heel and fist, hair, follicles without hair, pores, moles, freckles. . .and memories.

I tried to remember what the dragon on the back of Günter's hand looked like. I thought it was more of the variety that knights slew than the Oriental kind. He had the dragon tucked between his legs at that moment and I wanted to go over and get a better look at it, but decided I'd better do it by memory.

I was the White Knight. Günter was the Black Knight. I think he was the Black Knight. I never got to actually see under his helmet, so I can't be sure. We were about to joust. For real. In a tournament with thousands of spectators, including a king, a queen and a prince. I was the popular knight and got all the applause. The prince even threw me a white rose which I tucked into my helmet for luck. The Black Knight got all the boos. He looked evil. He was in black armor, of course, and he was bigger and stronger and meaner and he had a horse that was also bigger and stronger and meaner. But I was sure to win. The good guys always win. I had Right on my side. And the prince.

We rode out to the center of the arena, lances held high in salute to their majesties and, for protocol, to each other. As we passed each other on the way to our starting points, I could've sworn he winked at me. I don't know how I thought I saw him wink since he had his helmet on, but I knew it all the same. I thought maybe he wanted a tryst after our joust. Sounded fine to me. I made up my mind not to hurt him too much in the joust so he'd be in better condition later. I needn't have concerned myself. He clobbered me on the first pass. I was out cold and he went off with their majesties . . . all three of them!

Just once, I'd like to win one of these things!

The dragon never did show up.

Next thing I remember, the conductor was shaking me and asking for the *billetas*. I got mine out and woke up Günter to get his. It was still dark outside.

"Is anything wrong?" I asked in English, still too groggy to know where I was or what language we were doing at the moment. I had a slight feeling that we were someplace we weren't supposed to be.

"Oh, do you speak English, señor?" the conductor asked me.

"Yes. Do you?" I told you I wasn't awake yet.

"Oh yes, sir. I spent four years in the United States of America working on a very big water dam and I was even younger than you are now. I was not allowed to take my wife with me because of the difficult working conditions and the shortages of living spaces, so I. . . ."

"Why are you checking our tickets in the middle of the night?" Günter asked.

"I'll bet you think it is because you are in the second-class car with only third-class tickets. Don't you? This is not it at all. I thought you might be on the wrong train and. . ."

"Wrong train?" I was starting to wake up.

"You see, I saw you sneak in here to sleep earlier tonight and I told myself at that time that I should be sure to wake you up when we left the other cars behind in Zaragoza, but I forgot to wake you up

over on my side, facing away from him. I grabbed the side of the mattress, praying it would keep me there all night.

Even from the other side of the bed, I was aware how clean he smelled. How could anyone smell clean after that train ride? I didn't. I had noticed his smell before, just from standing next to him on the hill that night and then again when we slept on the *Santa María*. Before I went into a coma, that is. There was a real freshness about him that I couldn't identify. I didn't smell any of the colognes or deodorants or any of the usual crap people foul up the air with. But he had no real body odor either. Just clean. It was intoxicating.

It lulled me to sleep.

8. Spies!

It started in a barrel. Only this time, I wasn't alone in there! Richie Cunningham from "Happy Days" was in the barrel with me. I think we were hiding from Potsie. Or maybe the Fonz. I'm not sure. Ralph wasn't there. Maybe I was Ralph. I hope not.

I wondered later, if I had to be in a barrel with an actor, why it couldn't have been someone like Matt Dillon or, if it had to be a "Happy Days" character, Scott Baio. Ron Howard isn't bad, I guess, but I can't help but remember him as Opie on the old "Andy Griffith Show." I'm surprised 'Aint' Bea wasn't in the damn barrel, too!

Anyway, there we were in the barrel, Richie and I, sort of half-wrapped around each other, face-to-face. I willed myself to move in the dream and suddenly, we were mutually face-to-crotch. If you're going to be jammed into a barrel with someone, you might as well make the best of it, I always say. Just as I was snuggling in nice and comfortable, Potsie lifted the lid off the barrel and said, "Hi guys!"

We chased him for six blocks, to someone's house. We went in. They were having a huge cocktail party and there were thousands of champagne glasses covering the floor of the main room. Waiters were pouring strawberry Kool-Aid into the glasses and we had to walk on the rims of the glasses to get out to the terrace where all the people were.

Everyone was talking about some homicidal maniac that had been on a killing spree all over the town, crashing big cocktail parties and wiping out the guests. Somehow I knew who he was and I was in love with him.

The doors flew open in the main room and there he was! The mass murderer! Crashing the party! No one said anything. They just kept chatting away and sipping on their little red drinks. The killer picked up a glass from the floor, took a sip out of it, threw the glass into the fireplace and walked toward the terrace. I froze. Everyone was carrying on like nothing was wrong and this guy was walking right up to me! I gulped. He reached into his jacket and pulled out a. . . .

I woke up.

I quickly checked to see if I was still on my own side of the bed. I was. I went back to sleep.

And to the party. I don't have the faintest idea why I wanted to go back to that dream with a murderer standing there about to kill me or whatever he was going to do. Love, I guess. My lover, the killer, was gone. So were Richie and Potsie. Grant and Jeanie were there in their places. And the champagne glasses were gone from the floor of the main room. I think it was a different house.

Grant, Jeanie and I walked out to the lawn area and sat down at a card table with Günter. I think it was canasta we were playing. Jeanie said something about how pretty the big white clouds were out over the ocean. I told her that it wasn't clouds at all, that it was soapsuds.

"Oh."

Someone dealt the next hand and we resumed our game. I think it was still canasta.

"Damn. They're getting closer!" I said. "I guess we'll have to finish the game inside."

"They're coming from Los Angeles," someone observed. I don't know what city we were in, but I guess it was close to Los Angeles.

"The Russians," I supposed.

"Oh."

We picked up our cards and walked toward the house. It was a different house.

The soapsuds covered the entire horizon and were cascading over some tall office buildings off in the distance. They seemed to be moving rapidly toward us. We barely made it inside before the bubbles hit the roof and engulfed the house. We ran around closing windows and doors and cupboards. I don't know why we were closing cupboards.

"We'd better turn on the TV," someone said, "and see what's going on."

"No electricity!" I shouted as everything went to black.

And I woke up.

I was lying up against Günter with my head on his shoulder and my hand on his chest. I wondered if I was awake or if I was finally having a decent dream.

I was awake.

I told myself to move away from there immediately, but I didn't do it. I asked myself why I was putting myself through all this torture. Myself didn't know. I slid my hand down to his stomach and played with the little hairs that ran down from his belly button to you-know-where. You-know-where is where I wanted to go. But I didn't. I don't know why. Scared to, I guess. I kept telling myself that I'd rather be with him as a friend than not be with him at all, which is what I figured would happen if I kept that up. I took my erection and went back to my side of the bed, went back to sleep and went back to that dream.

We were waist-deep in soapsuds. Günter was gone! Grant, Jeanie and I searched the house for him. It was a different house, again. We didn't find him.

Günter had been kidnaped! I got hysterical!

Jeanie told me to water the flowers.

"What flowers?" I demanded.

"The ones in your hand," she said.

Sure enough, there was a bouquet of flowers coming out of the palm of my hand. They were silk. Some were red, but most of them were blue. They looked like a feather duster. I bent my hand slightly and the flowers disappeared, leaving only a small black cone in the middle of my palm. I opened my hand out flat again and the flowers came back. I bent my hand and they went away. I lifted the little black cone out of my palm and examined it. It was spongy and, as much as I squeezed it and pulled on it and pushed on it, the flowers wouldn't appear. There was a cone-shaped hole in my palm. I didn't like that at all, so I replaced the little black cone in the hole. I opened my hand out flat and the flowers popped out. I watered them.

Günter was being held prisoner in the garage by Americans who were Russian spies! The soapsuds had just been a diversion so they could get Günter out of there undetected. They thought he was a famous German scientist and they were torturing him to get him to confess to something or other. They were yelling at him and beating him and calling him names. I was distraught.

"I've got to save him!" I cried.

Grant and Jeanie tried to hold me back, but I broke away from them and smashed through the door and into the garage, which became a basement.

They weren't Americans who were Russian spies. They were Russians who were American spies who thought Günter was a German Russian spy, posing as a famous American scientist.

I pleaded with them to let him go!

They laughed at me.

"He isn't who you think he is!" I told them.

"Who are you?" one of them asked me.

"I don't know, but I do know that he isn't who you think he is."

"Prove it!" one of them said.

"Where is he?" I asked.

They showed me to a corner of the basement room and there, lying in a heap on an old mattress, was a very beat up lump. I couldn't recognize him like that!

"I can't tell by looking at him; you've messed him up too much. I'll have to make love to him," I said.

Suddenly, Günter and I were alone. In bed. In our underwear. I moved over close to him. It smelled like Günter all right. Clean.

I put my hand on his belly and tested the little hairs below his navel. It must be him, I thought.

I snapped the elastic on his combination swimwear and underpants. Definitely red.

I stuck my hand down inside his pants. Nothing! It wasn't there!

"What have you done with his cock?!!"

He rolled over.

Ahh!

Ummmmmmmm.

"Hey!" He wacked me across the back of the head.

"Uh wmf dwvmngg," I said, swallowing.

"What the hell do you think you are doing?" he asked.

"I don't know," I said. "I was asleep. Apparently I was sucking your dick." I must've thought I was still in the dream or I wouldn't have been that brave.

"Fucker," he muttered as he adjusted his swimwear underpants and got out of bed.

"I was dreaming. I swear."

He took a cigarette from the pack on the dresser and lit it. . .being careful not to look at me.

"Günter, I. . ."

"Leave me alone."

"I didn't mean for that to happen. I was asleep. I was dreaming that you were kidnaped by spies and that they were beating you up. And the only way they would let you go was if I proved to them that you weren't who they thought you were and you were so beat up that I couldn't recognize you so I had to make love to you. It was the only way I could be sure it was you!"

"Are you crazy?" he asked, rhetorically.

Yes. I wouldn't believe that story either if I were you. But it was all true. I don't know where it came from. I don't know where any of the weird stuff in my head comes from.

"Do you think I am stupid?" he asked.

"No. But it is the truth. You can believe it or not. I'm going back to sleep." I pulled the covers up over my head, closed my eyes as tight as I could and scooted as far as possible to the edge of the bed, facing the wall.

I heard him put his cigarette out in the ashtray. Then nothing for a moment. I guessed that he was looking out the window. I wondered if he would do anything about what had just happened. Like hit me. Or, worse yet, leave me.

He got back into bed, giving the blankets a hefty tug. I guess I had yanked them too far when I pulled them up over my head.

I could hear him breathing.

I wanted to speak, but couldn't.

I wanted to touch him, but wouldn't.

I wondered if he really was asleep while I was going down on him.

He rolled onto his side. I tensed, afraid he might speak. If he was going to leave me in the morning, I did not want to know it.

I tried to figure out that strange dream, those strange dreams, but the only part of the whole mess that made any sense to me at all was the maddening frustration that had been building up in me from wanting to make love to him. Sure was a roundabout way to get there.

Günter was snoring gently.

Then Life gave me still another of its little reminders that I must never take it too seriously: I let a fart. A near lethal one. Well actually, I didn't let it—it got away before I was even aware of its impending escape.

Farting with your head under the covers falls in the same category as dropping the toilet seat on your penis—limited primarily to five-to-seven-year-old boys and drunks on their knees—both of which I have personal knowledge. The category is *stupid*. As kids we had a word for such nerdness. The word was Queech. Plural: Queechae. If I ever knew the origin of the word, I've forgotten it since, but one of the popular definitions going around was that a Queech was a person who farts in the bathtub and then bites at the bubbles.

Farting in bed is also a foolproof test to determine if your sleepmate is really out or not—you get yelled at or hit if (s)he's still awake—although that was not my purpose at the time. Günter was definitely asleep.

I pulled the covers down to get some air.

I listened to his soft snore. It was soothing. I knew I would miss that sound in the nights to come.

I started thinking about how this trip was the most masochistic thing I had ever put my psyche through. I began to wonder if there was some deep, psychological need I had developed to punish myself for something. Was I testing some particular trait in my character? Which?

If I was, I had failed. Or my subconscious had failed anyway. I moved away from him earlier when I woke up. My subconscious is the one that put me back over there to get into trouble. They say dreams are our release valve to keep us from going bonkers. I wondered if I would've gone stark-raving mad during the night if I hadn't had that dream. I wondered if I was going to go mad anyway.

I wondered if my balls were going to hurt as much in the morning as they did the last time I'd slept with Günter. Just the thought of all that pain caused me to wince. One pair of blue balls in a week was enough!

I was still erect from the dreamsuck. I wondered if he had noticed it when he was yelling at me. The blankets had been pulled down and I was sitting there sticking out for all the world to see. Oh god, I thought, I hope he didn't notice my underpants! It was pretty dark in the room, but the moonlight was streaming in through the window and I could see him clearly. He wasn't looking at me though. Good.

I thought I felt a little pain beginning to stir in the gonads ("gonies" as we kids used to say and then giggle). I didn't want to go through that again!

I had previously, although unintentionally, determined that Günter was sound asleep and so, remembering the old adage, "An ounce of prevention is worth a pound of cure," I slipped silently off the side of the bed, grabbed an old sock and did myself an ounce of prevention.

Good night.

9. Silence May Be Golden, But . . .

My nuts didn't hurt when I woke up the next morning, but there was enough attitude in that room to serve four and still have leftovers for later in the week.

He was dressed, repacked and ready to go.

I was in bed, undressed and unrepacked.

"Are you ready?" he asked me.

Do I look like I'm ready? I was already starting to think I should have let the spies keep him.

"Give me five minutes," I said. I swung my legs off the edge of the bed and quickly pulled my pants on, kicking a sock under the bed as I stood up.

Günter folded his arms across his chest, leaned against the dresser and watched me.

I splashed water on my face at the little sink in the corner of the room and then brushed my teeth.

Günter unfolded his arms, lit a cigarette and watched me.

I grabbed fresh socks and a shirt from one of my suitcases and finished dressing.

Günter pulled a chair out, sat on it and watched me.

I closed my bags and put them by the door.

"Do I have time to take a piss?" I asked.

He said nothing.

I went down the hall to the toilet. When I got back to the room, the door was ajar and Günter was gone.

I picked up by bags and ran down the hall and to the stairs. Well, actually, I picked up the bags and made about two steps and dropped one of them. I picked it up and promptly dropped another one. It took about five tries before I got it right. Well, actually, I never did get it right, but I did get me and my luggage down to the lobby area. One of the suitcases went down the stairs ahead of me, but it was where I needed it to be, so what the hell.

There was no one around downstairs and we'd paid for the room the night before, so I left without saying good-bye to our hosts. I could see Günter on the train platform as I stepped out the front door. The inn was that close to the tracks.

He was sitting on the platform, leaning back against his pack, gazing down the tracks. The morning sun had just cleared the distant hills and it was sitting right on the train tracks at the bottom of the V-neck pass we'd be rattling through in less than an hour. The sun was hitting Günter's back and I could feel the warmth penetrating his sweater. He sat up straighter to get more of the sun, then turned to face it. He became a golden statue.

It was one of the many times I've wished I were an artist. I pictured myself seated on a little stool at my easel there in the middle of Bobadilla's plaza. My fellow villagers would stop to say hello and peer over my shoulder to admire my devotion to the "Golden Boy on the Platform." Year after year this would go on, always the same painting, always waiting for him to return. I would be the Delta Dawn of the Bobadilla art set.

But instead of easel, stool and paints, I had three rapidly deteriorating suitcases . . . one of which had just smashed my left foot on its way to the plaza bricks.

It came open.

And the train was pulling up to the platform.

And I couldn't get the damned suitcase closed.

And the train came to a stop.

And I still couldn't get the bag closed.

And Günter was getting on the train! He looked back at me as he stepped up into the car. It wasn't an angry look, but it wasn't a particularly friendly one either. I like to think he was as confused as I was at that moment.

I didn't blame him for being upset. Whether Günter was awake or asleep, I had taken it upon myself to use him. And it didn't matter that I was asleep when I used him—the act was reality even if the circumstances weren't. As I said, I didn't blame him for being upset. I just wanted some help with my baggage.

Suddenly the man and woman from the inn appeared at my side. He closed the one suitcase and then carried them all over to the train. She brought me out of my daze and led me onto the train, handing me a small lunch basket as we began to pull away. We waved at each other. I think I overdid it with the *graciases*. Two, three, even ten probably would've been enough and the last seven or so were lost completely as we entered the tunnel at the edge of the village.

The train wasn't as crowded as it was on our previous third-class experience, so it was a little more comfortable. I guess everyone else had eaten breakfast already because they turned down my offers of food. Günter and I had a feast. Without speaking, of course. There was fruit, bread and cheese in the center of the basket. Then at one end there was a cold ceramic jug of orange juice. At the other end were warm boiled eggs, coffee and meat pastries. The meat things were like pigs-in-a-blanket except they were nothing like pigs-in-a-blanket. It was delicious and quite satisfying, even if we were eating like cloistered monks.

I was sitting between Günter and another man. The man had an aura of peace about him. It was a warm glow—I could actually feel it. It relaxed me. We didn't speak. He had his eyes closed, but he wasn't sleeping. I closed my eyes too and tried to concentrate on him. I wanted to have a fantasy about him, but it wouldn't come. I just got calmer and soft-warm.

I've had that happen to me a few times since then, but that morning was the first time I'd ever basked in the aura of a stranger and I felt good about it all day. He was still sitting like that when Günter and I had to change to the southbound train. Nothing was ever said between us and we never made eye contact, so the spell wasn't broken.

The train going south was half empty, so Günter and I had a compartment to ourselves—he on one side, me on the other. People came and went at the many stops along the way, but we were alone most of the time. And he slept most of the time.

Between my little naps, I again had to resort to self-amuse and, since I refused to let Günter play in any of my fantasies, I thought about Charley. I hadn't seen Charley since ninth grade. He had gotten very heavy into pills and acid, so his parents took him off someplace and none of them ever came back. I wondered what he looked like and what he was doing with his life . . . if he was still alive.

I pictured myself alone in a first-class compartment. I think it was on the Orient Express. My porter had just left the room after making up my bed and pouring my brandy. I changed into my smoking jacket, prepared my pipe and, just as I was about to light it, there was a knock.

It was the porter. There had been some mix up with the reservations and an American serviceman had been left without quarters for the night. The porter thought, my being an American too, that I might be willing to let the man sleep in the other bed in my compartment. Of course. Anything for an American serviceman.

The porter brought the man into the room. He was about my age and size and very good-looking. He was in full-dress uniform. He looked familiar.

We stared at each other.

"Tad?"

"Yeah?"

"Don't you recognize me?"

"Sort of."

"It's me, Charley!"

"Charley!"

We embraced. Manly. You know, patting each other vigorously on the back like bears. The porter, who was making up the other bunk, was just beaming with pride that he had been responsible for reuniting two old friends.

Then Charley kissed me . . . passionately.

The porter lost his beam. "Goddamn!" he said. "I go through all the work of making up this other bed and now I suppose you ain't even gonna use it!"

I told him he was right and slipped him a fifty-dollar bill to get his beam back and get the hell out!

At that point, I either fell asleep or lost sanity because the daydream got out of control.

As soon as the porter left, I began to undress.

"I've been looking for you for years," Charley told me.

"I've thought about you a lot too," I said, ripping the last of my clothes off and throwing them across the room.

He pulled out a pistol.

"What the hell are you doing?" I screamed.

"Blowing your fucking brains out, asshole!"

"Why?"

Boy was I pissed off. It's bad enough that my head gets me into these things, but to drop it up in the air like that, to leave things hanging, to end up with a why? without an answer is infuriating as hell! My guess is that he probably pulled the trigger and my brain said "forget it" and woke me up. I always wake up just before getting killed or seriously hurt in dreams. It must be a built-in defense mechanism. I often wonder if I would actually die if some subconscious wiring got crossed and a death dream accidentally went all the way. Of course if it did, I wouldn't be able to share this great insight with the world because I'd be dead. Maybe people who die in their sleep are murdered in a dream. The autopsy wouldn't show anything. If I believed in seances, I could ask someone. But I don't. So I can't.

I wondered why Charley had wanted to kill me. But then I realized Charley wasn't really there so I had to wonder why I thought Charley would want to kill me. Fortunately, we arrived at our destination before I had time to further confuse myself pursuing that one.

La Linea. The Line. The borderline to the great Rock of Gibraltar. Gateway to Africa!

Without speaking, Günter and I left the train.

In silence we walked to the center of the town.

With minimal and polite conversation, we got a room with two beds in a *pensión*.

And polite we remained for our three days there with our separate beds, separate meals, separate walks and separate depressions.

At least I think he was depressed, too. He was even quieter than usual. He stayed away from the room for hours and when he wasn't gone I was, so we saw very little of each other.

We did do our laundry together on the roof that first afternoon. In a washtub. With a washboard. Dry on the line. That great Mediterranean sun made the clothes smell terrific.

I had taken to muttering. With no one to talk to, my conversations with myself were getting longer and more frequent and too often aloud . . . like those crazy people you see on the street and make fun of. I was like that. At one point during the washing, I was thinking about something to do with the laundry and the roof, but what came out of my mouth was sort of a bark:

"Roof . . . roofroof . . . roofroofroof."

"What?" he asked.

"Nothing," I said.

I felt like an idiot. I wanted to crawl in a hole for barking like that. In front of him. But I couldn't crawl in a hole because we were on a roof . . . roofroof.

That was one of our longer discussions while we were in La Linea.

We almost had an argument the second day we were there. I tried to start one. I said, "Good Morning!" in sort of a singsong way— happylike. He opened his mouth to speak, then thought better of it and walked out the door. He looked like he was about to yell at me. I wanted him to yell at me. It wouldn've made me feel better. Getting yelled at was such an integral part of my childhood that I often do things just to get yelled at. I thought for sure my cheerful greeting would set him off. Too bad.

I asked myself why I was playing out this farce. I didn't know, still.

Or at least I didn't understand it at the time because what I was doing was treating the whole thing like a lovers' quarrel with the idea that it would soon pass and everything would be all right. Just like married people do. Schizo.

He did bring back a *churro* for me from one of his walks. A *churro* is sort of a rope doughnut. In the States, it's usually just a stick, but in La Linea it's a spiral. They cook them right on the street carts so they're always fresh and hot. The literal translation of *churro* is "fritter." Interestingly, it is used vulgarly as "turd" and sometimes "prick."

"Thanks for the *churro*," I said.

"*Bitte*," he said.

"Are we still going to Morocco together?" I asked.

"I do not know," he answered and left again.

Something very wrong was going on inside my body . . . inside my head. I felt different physically as though my body chemistry had changed somehow. I knew it had something to do with that night with Günter in Bobadilla, but I wasn't sure what. I could actually feel my body parts . . . and I don't mean by touch . . . I mean that I was aware of them, consciously aware of their presence, something that usually only happens when there's pain. I could feel the back of my throat without closing it. I could feel my diaphragm without holding my breath or hiccuping. I could feel my cock without tensing the piss-cut-off muscles. I could feel my anus without tightening the sphincter. I could even feel my toes as individuals without wiggling them.

And they all demanded attention. And not just by touch. They all wanted pressure. Firm, lasting pressure. Weight.

It scared me.

I tried writing my feelings down in a journal, hoping to arrive at some understanding of what was happening to me, but I still couldn't make much sense of it. In the past, I'd always made fun of my sexual frustrations, but I couldn't intellectualize it that time.

And it got even weirder. I read my copy of "Afrika" over and over . . .

> His million fingers caress my body,
>   covering me with his fevered warmth.
> He engulfs my groin, suffocates my soul.

and even though I'd written the poem myself and it gave me some consolation, I couldn't relate to the fact that I had actually written it. I even copied it over into the journal . . .

> He mounts me—intent on his cruel rape—
> his crushing weight upon my chest.
> He devours me as we begin our loving thrust.

and still felt estranged from it . . . as though some other writer were trying to explain to me how I felt and I wasn't getting the message!

I tried writing specifically about that night, what I felt afterwards, what I thought he felt afterwards, but the only detail I could fix in my mind was the moment when he hit me on the back of the head . . . the moment when reality hit me in the stomach. Then I remembered beating off on the floor next to the bed . . . into a sock . . . and I remembered that I had felt humiliated and I was angry with him for what I had done to myself. I concentrated on that anger. I felt that anger in my bowels. I felt it in my groin. I felt it in my stomach. I felt blood surging through my body . . . warm, soothing, throbbing . . . into my temples, into my hands and feet, into my penis.

An image popped into my head: Thousands of boys, men and old geezers all beating off at the same time, each with their own individual style. I can't explain how the image worked because those thousands all existed at the exact same moment in time, but not like those split screen things they do in movies. They were just all there at once. My guess is that it was some other dimension, one we can't or don't know how to use in our limited, material world.

I started giggling at the image. Some of them were pretty silly looking . . . a lot of strange techniques, I thought. I tried to verbalize that image into my journal, but it got ridiculous. It made me think of my very first journal. It had a lot of masturbation stuff in it. I was about fifteen, I think, and I was sure the Mother was sneaking into my room to read it while I was at school, so I added a preface:

> "May God damn to hell anyone who would intrude on this account without my personal invitation. You would be trespassing on my rights as a human being. You would be a geek who

stepped off the last rung of the ladder, preparing to eat your first live chicken."

At fifteen, I often thought of stuff like worms feeding on people's hearts and earwigs boring into brains and snakes crawling around in bowels, so I threw some of that in too! And then, with the vision of the Mother turning purple, I added:

"Which would you rather do? Slide down a forty-foot razor blade? Suck on a gorilla's nose till his head caves in? Or have your balls smashed with a hundred-pound sledge hammer?"

I was sorry to leave the women out of that third one, but we didn't tell jokes like that to girls when I was a teenager, so most of them only included boy parts. I couldn't even think of a female equivalent that conjures up that much pain. Maybe getting your tits caught in the proverbial wringer? Not equivalent.

I knew that my little preface wouldn't stop the Mother from reading my journal, but I enjoyed the idea of her seeing the curse the next time she decided to butt into my private life. I even put a note on the margin of the current entry, saying, "See Preface!" I started leaving the journal out on top of my desk to entice her—willing to sacrifice my privacy—because I wanted so much to fuck her mind over.

On the third day in La Linea, I woke at sunrise and decided to go for a walk. I bought a *churro y café* and headed for the country.

La Linea wasn't anywhere near as large as Barcelona, but it was still a decent walk to the town limits. The old buildings shank from three stories to two to one to lean-to.

There were hundreds of cardboard shanties on the beach! I couldn't believe what I was seeing! They started just at the edge of an aqueduct that fed into the ocean and stretched for a mile down the beach. The first row of shacks was about twenty yards from the water and there were at least a dozen more rows of them behind that. It was the most depressing sight I'd ever seen.

People were clothed in rags. Naked and dirty kids. Shanties with six or seven or more people living in them. Bony dogs.

It was low tide and the sand down by the water had little piles of human shit all over it. High tide would be their flush. I wondered if they wiped and, if they did, what they used. An old man was squatting near the water, dropping one *churro* at a time, then waddling a few inches forward before dropping the next one. Then he just sat there and waited for a wave to come rushing up around is ankles. He splashed some water on his ass, pulled up his pants, called his dog and walked back up into the cardboard ghetto.

My emotions were playing roller coaster. My self-pity washed out to sea with that old man's shit. Words like aghast, awed, humbled, confused and pity came to mind, but were not adequate.

It was a religious experience for me! I imagined a cult arising! It would begin with a popular, but subversive, novel titled *The Old Man and the Shit*. The first small sect would form and call itself "The Church of the Golden Churro." There would be an ornate, solid gold Churro on the altar and everybody would wear one on a chain around his(er) neck.

New words came to mind: injustice, inequality, immorality, inhumanity!

I wanted to go in there—into that handmade hell, but language or no language, there was no way I could speak to those people. I knew nothing of such poverty. I wasn't qualified.

I ran away.

Günter was acting weird when I got back. He seemed almost happy to see me. I'd gone out that morning before he woke up and I got the feeling he thought maybe I wasn't going to be coming back. He didn't say that, but he did ask if I wanted to go up on the roof . . . roofroof . . . and get some sun.

We stretched out on towels about eight or ten feet from each other. He still had his tan. I was still white-gray-beige. The sun was hot and piercing. He tossed me a bottle of suntan lotion, but didn't offer to help me put it on. I didn't ask.

"Where did you go this morning!?" he asked.

"Just for a walk," I told him.

He waited for me to continue, but that's all I had to say. He rolled over onto his stomach and turned his head the other way. I don't know what was wrong with me. I knew he was ready to talk finally, but then I wasn't ready. Pout for pout. Stupid. It's bad enough to be stupid and not know that you're being stupid, but to be stupid and know that you're being stupid and still be stupid is really stupid.

I turned to look at him. What the hell were we playing? What did he want? What did I want? How do you tell the difference between love and lust at the beginning of a relationship? I confused myself even further by thinking that maybe I really didn't love him because I wanted to go over there and attack him. It made me feel guilty. My erection made me feel guilty.

I never felt guilty with Charley. It was all so natural with Charley.

I remember the time we went on a camping trip with our Sunday School class and our teacher said that Charley and I couldn't share a tent because we always goofed off and made too much noise. He put Charley in his tent with him and put this really wimpy kid (a Queech if there ever was one) in with me. Charley and I suspected that the teacher had something else in mind—something like playing around with Charley—because he was always touching Charley and putting his arm around him and patting him on the knee and stuff like that.

Charley and I made a plan. Dinner was hot dogs, cole slaw and pork-and-beans. We ate double of everything. Triple on the beans. I used to carry a bag of radishes around with me all the time for snacks (I started out on onions, but the Mother made me give them up, so I switched to radishes) and we ate my whole weekend supply that first night. Oh . . . and we stole a bunch of boiled eggs from one of the other kids and ate them too.

As soon as I got into the tent, I pretended to be straightening out my sleeping bag, bent way over, and blew a fart into the wimp's face that would've put a camel into a coma. He started screaming and crying and ran off to the teacher's tent where Charley had begun a more subtle approach—silent bombers! I ran after the wimp and, just as we got there, the teacher was throwing open his tent flaps to get some air!

It was pretty dark out there, but I could've sworn I spotted a boner poking at teacher's pants.

"He farted in my face!" the wimp cried.

"You mean he passed gas," teach corrected. I gassed him all right . . . but good. And from the nauseated look on teach's face, I guessed Charley had managed to get his guts even rottener than mine.

"What I mean is that he farted! In my face!" the wimp insisted.

"Go back to sleep! All of you!" teacher yelled. The whole camp was up by then, trying to find out what happened.

"Who farted?" one of them asked.

"Whose face?" another shouted.

"Go to bed!" teach tried again.

"I won't," the wimp whimpered.

"All right, Oliver, you can stay with me. Charley you go with Tad and I don't want to hear any noise out of you two! Is that clear?"

"Yessir!"

We ran to our tent as fast as we could, trying to hold our laughter till we got there and got the flaps closed.

It hurt.

"It worked!" Charley said, laughing and farting.

"Did you see how green he was?" I laughed and farted.

"God that stinks!"

"Yeah!"

We rolled on our sleeping bags and on each other.

"Sh," he said, settling down.

"Sh," I said, settling down.

My stomach hurt. I stretched out on my back with my hands behind my head, gasping for air.

Charley grabbed my T-shirt, pulled it up and then blew on my stomach like you do to babies, making a farting noise. We got hysterical again.

As I mentioned earlier, Charley was a late comer—so to speak—and we had been working diligently for the last two or three weeks trying to solve that problem. Everytime we were alone together, we worked on it.

I peeked out the tent flaps to make sure no one was spying on us and then tied them shut.

We got naked.

We had worked out a routine for Charley's debut. We always did me first, hoping it would serve as some kind of inspiration for Charley. That night I even tried out some of those funny little noises that Charley had made that time on his mother's new sofa. It was kind of fun. Twice he had to put his free hand over my mouth to shut me up. I bit his finger when I came!

We used my stuff to make him slippery. It helped. Charley said he knew something was different as soon as we got started. He had a couple of dry ones right away, but he said he wanted, had to keep going. Boy did he! It surprised both of us! Pop! I bet it would've gone ten feet in the air if the tent hadn't been there! He "left pecker tracks on the ceiling" as we kids used to say and then giggle.

"Bar mitzvah!" Charley shouted. He had just turned thirteen that week.

"Sh!" I told him and started giggling again.

It took both of our T-shirts to wipe up all that stuff. We buried them. And parents think kids lose their clothes at camp! The truth is that the mountains have been planted with hundreds of complete wardrobes!

Lying on my back, on the rooftop of a La Linea *pensión*, I imagined all those clothes beginning to grow! "Just beyond the Monterey pines over there," the ranger giving the tour would say, "you'll see a grove of size twelve T-shirts. The low-growing plants you see near them are jockey short shrubs."

A huge glob of pre-come had oozed through the material of my shorts and was just sitting there in a perfect bubble, glistening in the sun. I rolled over quickly and looked to see if Günter was still facing the other way.

He was gone.

10.   A Ferry Story

The days which followed, or rather the frustrations contained therein, inspired me to write:

THE TOILET

Someone decides to knock
   on the door
And a cockroach scurries
   'cross the floor.

The phone begins to ring
   off the wall
And a spider sneaks in
   from the hall.

Suddenly there's a crack
   in the seat
And the tissue's down to
   the last sheet.

But the very worst yet,
   the acme,
      the summit!
Is when you realize
   you're about
      to vomit!
And it's all because you
   sat down on
      the Toilet!

—Tad Prescott

Here's what happened. I woke up that next morning with the worst case of the trots I'd ever experienced. And, true to form, the nausea hit right in the middle of my evacuation. Fortunately, there was a wash basin crowded right up against the toilet in that tiny little hallway bathroom. It was no great joy cleaning it up, but that was a hell of a lot better than it would've been had I puked on the floor between my feet. All the time I'd been in Europe, I had not had even the slightest bit of trouble—solid as the Rock of Gibraltar, so to speak—and I had been drinking the water and eating salads and everything. Then, I had to go and have bean soup for dinner the night before we were leaving for Casablanca . . . on bicycles!

"Bicycles?!" I gasped.

"Sure. Why not?" Günter said.

"You want us to ride all the way to Casablanca on bicycles? One-speed bicycles? Through I don't know how many miles of isolated Moroccan countryside? In the heat of summer?" (Just the two of us?) "Okay."

I had gone back down to the room after the sunning session on the roof. I showered and changed clothes and then while I was washing the stain out of the crotch of my shorts in the wash basin, Günter returned. He was excited.

"Guess what I bought," he said.

"What?"

"Come downstairs and see."

"Just tell me." I wasn't sure I was ready for him to be in such a good mood.

"Come on!" he said and dragged me out of the room, down the stairs and out onto the street.

"See!"

"See what?" All I saw was the usual vending carts and street sweepers and two bicycles someone had left leaning against the side of the building.

"The bikes!" he said.

Oh god, I thought, they're ours.

The first thing we had to do was dump my luggage and two-thirds of the crap I was carrying around with me. We bought an old knapsack from a junk dealer. When we got back to the room Günter decided he'd make biking shorts for us. Two pairs of pants got amputated and cuffed. To me they looked more like moutain climbing shorts than biking shorts, but then I didn't know what biking shorts were supposed to look like. He did look like a Tyrolean mountain climber . . . in a menthol cigarette ad. I looked like the remains he would be digging out of the avalanche.

Günter treated for dinner to celebrate our next-day departure. I decided that Kaiser Wilhelm must've given him a lot more money than he was telling me about. Either that or he robbed the guy. Anyway, that's when I had the bean soup . . . and the rest is history.

I wobbled back to the room on weakened knees after my bout with the toilet and the wash basin. We were going to be leaving in a few minutes . . . me with diarrhea and nausea. Terrific. Günter was bubbly. I was yellow-green.

Fortunately for me it was a very short ride to the ferry landing. Let me put that another way. He rode. I walked, pushing my bike.

The ferry was huge. It held thousands of people and maybe hundreds of cars and trucks. Animals, too. They let us lock our bicycles in a storage room so we wouldn't have to be watching them the whole trip. We were in third-class, which was just about at the waterline and had windows that did not open. No air. At all. We went up on deck.

The wind was cold, but it felt great. I was beginning to feel better, even a little hungry. We bought cheese sandwiches and Pepsis from a dwarf who was running around on deck with a basket bigger than she was.

Speaking of baskets. For some reason, Günter was showing one that day and he usually didn't. It was driving me crazy! I wondered if he had altered the crotch on his shorts somehow while he was sewing up the cuffs. He sure as hell didn't alter mine.

Grant used to show a basket all the time. I used to have a thing for Grant. I also used to have a thing for Jeanie. In fact, Jeanie and I were sleeping together when we met Grant at college. I was still playing pecker-n-pussy in those days.

Defining one's sexuality can be quite difficult for many people. I found it impossible. After Charley left town, I graduated to dating girls and pretty much stayed that way, with a few minor lapses, all the way through college and Jeanie. Then Grant came along and got me all confused again. Jeanie and I both got the hots for him. She told him. I did not. She won. I lost.

I didn't really lose, though, because we were a great threesome. We did everything together. Almost. Since they didn't know how I felt about Grant, they assumed the reason I was hanging around all the time was because I was still "carrying a torch" for Jeanie. That may have been part of it, but he was definitely the other part.

I finally told him how I felt. It was during one of our all-night talking sessions. Jeanie had crashed first and I had consumed a bottle and a half of courage—dry red. My confession didn't seem to bother him, but I noticed that we seldom had physical contact after that.

The night I crawled into bed with them, he got nervous because he thought I wanted him and she got nervous because she thought I wanted her when, in fact, I just couldn't stand to be alone that night. I don't know—maybe I wanted them both. Lonely gets weird sometimes. Besides, I was too drunk to do anything but sleep.

The night I crawled into bed with them was the night before we were supposed to leave for Hawaii, the night before I left for New York and eventually Europe.

I kept telling myself I should write to them, but I still hadn't figured out what to say. I did write to Stacey.

Ms. Stacey Randall
c/o Hotel Claire
(Next to "Moulin Rouge")
Casablanca, Morocco
Africa!
Hey Trish—
  We're on our way to you! You damn well better still be there! It may take a while. If we ever get off this slow ferry, we're taking bicycles! Do you believe that shit? So, anyway, get Casablanca ready for us. And see if you can find some <u>Absinthe.</u> I know it's illegal, but if it exists anywhere on this planet, it'll be in Casa

blanca. Gotta go now—we dock in an hour and I want to watch <u>my</u> continent as it looms up in the horizon.

Love ya,
Tadpole

P.S. Günter says hello.

I stayed glued to the rail on the top deck until we moored, just staring at Africa! It didn't look a damn bit different from the port we'd just left in Spain, but it felt a lot different.

Then I was ready . . . ready to touch the dark continent. Günter and I worked our way down the multitude of stairwells leading back to third-class where our bikes were stored. Apparently everyone had eaten big hearty breakfasts that morning before they boarded the ferry. I say that because they had thrown up those big hearty breakfasts all over the floor in the airtight third-class section—which turned out to be the only way off that damned boat! Slosh. Gag.

I posted the letter to Stacey and we hopped (he hopped, I eased) onto our bikes and headed down the road to Casablanca.

It was exhilarating! I hadn't ridden a bike since I got my driver's license at fifteen-and-a-half. It felt pretty good . . . even if it was a little harder to pump those pedals than I remembered. The air was so fresh, the sky so blue. The sun was bright, but not all that hot. The countryside was so . . . so . . . Southern California.

People waved at us as we rode by. One man in a horse cart even tossed us a couple of oranges, so we stopped at the next tree clump to eat them. The trees were at the edge of a cemetery. I told Günter how much I loved cemeteries. Günter told me that I was a strange person and that he would appreciate it very much if I didn't talk to him about dead people.

So I didn't tell him about one of my favorite games, The Graveyard Game. What you have to do is visit the grave of a stranger. You get 50 points just for having the nerve to be in a cemetery—100 if you go at night. Another 25 if you bring flowers—50 if you steal them from another grave. There are two directions you can go with the game once you have picked the dead person you want to visit. You can make up a history for him(er) to fit you or you can make up a history for yourself to fit him(er). The best way to decide is to read a few headstones to see if any are especially appealing or intriguing. You might find a kidnaper or a suicidee or a 108-year-old Tibetan alchemist that will stir your imagination. You lose 50 if you have to read more than five markers before you get the actual visit started. You gain 50 points if you start with the very first marker you walk up to. Score 25 if you kneel. Another 25 if you touch the marker and feel grief. Take 50 more if you get all choked up—100 if you actually sob out loud and get teary. Bonuses: Gain 100 if you honestly feel better as a human being when you leave. You lose 100 if you realize suddenly that you knew the dead person because you were supposed to be visiting a stranger and because you are callous and stupid to have forgotten him(er). Now the biggie: Score 1,000 points if a member of the deceased's family joins you at the grave and consoles you!

We finished eating our oranges and resumed our journey. We had probably gone only about six miles before stopping by the cemetery, and we only got about another five miles down the road before my back tire went flat! We had neither repair kit nor pump. Real smart, huh?

Luckily, I only had to push the damned thing a mile or two to the next little pocket of civilization—well, almost civilization. There were a half-dozen houses and about that many shops. No one spoke English, Spanish or German. We were able to act out our dilemma. No one had the wherewithal to fix a bike tire. Finally, we met a woman who directed us to a small farm on the far side of the village where the owner spoke Spanish.

Not only did the man speak Spanish, he also fixed flat bicycle tires. He also gave us a pump and some patches. He also invited us to spend the night in his house and took us to dinner at a neighbor's farm. He was your basic all-around Good Samaritan.

Our Samaritan was a retired Spaniard who had moved to Morocco after his wife died. The neighbors were a married French couple who were semiretired textbook writers.

The dinner was eight courses.

The best part of the evening was the conversation. If person 'A' speaks only French, person 'B' French and German, person 'C' French and Spanish, person 'D' Spanish and English, and person 'E' English and German . . . who conversed with whom? And who made the salad?

Every time one of us said something, it had to be translated around the table. After a few bottles of good wine, however, fewer and fewer translations happened and we were all just chatting away. I decided that people take language too literally—a person should stop trying to figure it all out and just sit back and let it happen. It worked! I poured myself another glass of wine, sat back in my chair, relaxed and thoroughly enjoyed a long exchange in French and German. I can't repeat what was said, but I knew what was going on at the time. Inflection, body language and intuition work well together if you let them.

Quite sated, we returned to the Samaritan's and sacked out. He had only one bedroom, so Günter and I got a Persian rug on the floor of the living room and a couple of blankets.

After my morning sickness, all that fresh air on the deck of the ferry and the bike ride/walk, I was exhausted and fell asleep immediately.

I was sitting in a full-lotus position (something I cannot do in real life) at the edge of a large body of water. I was dressed only in a loincloth and was staring directly into the sun (without sunglasses which is something else I cannot do in real life). The sun's reflection made a great fire in the rippling water. It was in that fire that my thoughts were focused. I felt a presence there—a truth, an enlightenment, something.

A small ferry or barge came out of the fire and drifted toward me. There was a man standing alone on the deck of the barge.

He stepped off the boat and walked across the water to me. (That was rapidly becoming my all-time favorite trick!)

Then I could see his face. He was the man from the train, the one I sat next to and basked in his aura. He had no eyes, but whatever was there wasn't like those white eyes they do in sci-fi movies. His eyes were nothing and everything at the same time.

He sat beside me and together we contemplated the great fire on the water. He passed on centuries of knowledge, all without saying a word.

I was enlightened!

Charley's body came floating to the surface of the water right in front of me. Then the Mother's body floated up. Then Stacey. Miken-Toby. Grant. Jeanie. Biff. Dierdre. My high school geometry teacher. And hundreds of others I didn't know. Finally Günter's body surfaced and it just lay there for a moment before sitting up, staring at me with dead eyes and reaching out to me!

I started crying.

I reached for him. I reached for all of them. I turned to the man from the barge to ask him what it meant, but he was gone. He was in the water with the others.

I wanted to be with them, but I couldn't move.

The tears were streaming down my face and I began to sob out loud.

Günter scooted over next to me on the floor and took me in his arms. He wiped the tears from my cheeks and pulled me to his shoulder. He rubbed my temples.

"Just no spies tonight. Okay?" he whispered.

"Okay." I was crying again, but the new tears were much nicer ones.

11. Virus Poesis

I woke at sunrise the next morning feeling rested and rejuvenated. And smelling coffee. I jumped up from the floor, wrapped the blanket around my shoulders and said to myself:

> The butterfly swam
> through the rich colorful pools
> of its last sunset.

Well how nice for him, I thought, as I hurried off to the kitchen for that ever-important first cup of coffee. Señor Samaritan was sitting at the kitchen table with his coffee and a newspaper. He nodded good morning to me as though we had been roommates for years and indicated that I should help myself to the coffee. I did. He shoved a section of the paper over toward me as I sat down at the table. It was a Spanish newspaper. I wasn't that awake.

Then I remembered the dream. Jesus H. Ghandi! What a dream! I remembered Günter's consoling me. That was nice. I remembered being in his arms and not getting aroused. That was even nicer. Maybe I really did love him:

> Love wends its own way
> into places it well knows
> it ought not to go.

Where the hell did that come from? I asked myself. And the butterfly that swam by me when I got up? What is going on here?

Günter patted me on the shoulder as he walked by on his way to the coffeepot. I wondered if we, Günter and I, were starting one of those male bonding things I'd heard about.

The three of us cooked a huge breakfast and wolfed it down without much conversation. Good Sam threw about ten pounds of food into a gunnysack for us and Günter and I hit the old bike trail. Sam walked with us as far as the main road. We thanked him profusely for his aid and his hospitality and he wished us a safe journey, *vaya con Dios* and all that. I'll never forget his handshake. It was so . . . meaningful. Physically, it was like any other handshake, but emotionally, it had all the qualities of an embrace without the awkwardness that accompanies hugs between mere acquaintances. Don't get me wrong—I like hugs, crave them as a matter of fact, and think we ought to have them more often, but since that doesn't seem to be happening in our society, I wish we could warm up our handshakes with a little sincerity like Sam did.

It was a beautiful morning. The road was reasonably level, so the pedaling was easy. Günter was whistling. I was haikuing:

> The bird chased the cloud
> almost as far as the sky
> and never came back.

There it goes again, I thought. I looked at Günter to see if I had said that out loud. He wasn't looking at me, so he either didn't hear it or I said it to myself.

> The spider respun
> her path of silken beauty
> to devour her love.

Stop that! What is wrong with me? I felt my forehead. I was feverish. A virus maybe. *Virus poesis?* The dreaded poetry virus! Known to have driven thousands of would-be writers insane! No one is immune to the deadly germ! Ask any poetry editor. Housewives get it. Bankers get it. Runaway boys on bikes in Morocco get it! I should've been happy to get it, but it was scaring me. How long would it last? Would it get worse before it got better? Would it hurt?/Why is my back tire flat again?

I yelled at Günter who was a few yards ahead of me, still whistling. We pulled off the road and fixed my tire with the kit-and-pump Señor Samaritan had given us. I had picked up a nail. We were back in the saddle in less than thirty minutes.

I told myself to stop worrying about the strangeness coming out of my head. I thought maybe it had something to do with the dream I'd had the night before. Maybe that man I was meditating with had transmitted it all to me telepathically. Besides, I thought, it was just a little harmless haiku. As long as it didn't start in with more complicated stuff, there was nothing to worry about.

> Loving,
>   caring,
>   crying
>   Heart.
> Waning,
>   fighting,
>   losing
>   Hope.
> Hapless,
>   hopeless,
>   friendless
>   Soul.
> Trying,
>   growing,
>   winning
>   Love.

Oh shit! I shook my head trying to clear it. Fortunately I had another flat tire. It took my mind off it.

"Are you aiming for these nails?" Günter asked.

"No I am not!" I insisted, doubting myself.

That flat took a little longer—the patch wouldn't stick properly. There were only three patches left in the kit. I figured I'd better start watching what I was running over.

> "The summer sun warms
> the icy bitter sadness
> of your broken dreams."

I was glad it had gone back to just haiku. I was not glad, however, that I had apparently said that out loud.

"What did you say?" Günter asked me.

"I said: Winter makes its dreams
warm and cozy so that your
spirit won't get cold.'"

That isn't what I said!

"That isn't what you said," Günter said. "You said something about the summer sun."

"I know. I'm not well today."

We rode our bicycles through what was possibly the largest deposit of sandburs (we used to call them goatheads) ever deposited. Thousands! Millions! I had 243 of them in my front tire and 189 of them in my back tire. Günter had 317 in his front tire and 202 in his back tire. He won! 519 to 432 for a grand total of 951 holes. We had three patches. And hundreds of miles to go before we sleep.

We tried hitchhiking. No one would take the bikes. We didn't want to leave them behind because, even with flat tires, we could get something for them in Casablanca.

We tried pushing the bikes alongside us as we walked. It was much too difficult with all those sandburs and hot, flabby rubber front and back.

We tried marijuana. That worked. Good Samaritan slipped a couple joints to Günter before we left that morning.

What a man!

What a joint! I think it must've been the legendary Senegalese Thunderfuck I'd read about. We weren't all that far from Senegal. Out there in the wilderness. Alone on foot. Probably dying.

I saw a vulture.

Günter said I was hallucinating.

I was. I was ripped. I was wasted. I was out of it. I was dazed and confused. I was speaking Latvian!

Günter said something about gooseberries on the Eiffel tower.

Oh sure, blame it on the French, I thought, and then told him in Kurdish that there were no gooseberries on the Eiffel tower. They were elderberries.

He told me in Chinese that I as full of shit and did I want another drag?

Yes. It tasted like a Lucky Strike on a very hot day out behind Charley's dad's toolshed when we were fourteen. Lucky Strikes. L.S./M.F.T. Lucky Strike Means Fine Tobacco. L.S./M.F.T. Loose Straps Means Floppy Tits! LSMFT Lonely Spinsters Make Farts Too! LSMFT Loose Sacks Make Floppy Testicles! I sang:

> "Do your balls hang low?
> Can you rock 'em to and fro?
> Can you tie 'em in a knot?
> Can you tie 'em in a bow?
> Can you flop 'em o'er your shoulder
> Like a Continental soldier?
> Do your balls hang low?"

"You are hallucinating again," Günter said. "Your vulture is back!"

It was not. It was a pterodactyl!

I threw my poker chips at it. What poker chips? Oh, cookies. Apparently we had begun to eat from our bag of goodies from Goodie Sam. Chicken or maybe it was rabbit. Cheese. Bread. Apples or possibly pears. Maybe they were oranges—the skin was pretty tough. Günter wouldn't share his cookies with me. He said I threw mine at the vulture. Pterodactyl.

> "The sun painted sweet
>   on the tanned naked body
>   and gave it beauty." I said.

"Boy or girl?" Günter asked.

"How the hell am I supposed to know?! I am only the instrument here!"

I still had the munchies so I ate the rest of the white cheese. Günter made me spit it out by telling me some story about wanting to take a bath with it later. I wanted to go looking for the cookies I'd tossed. I took a little nap instead.

The bus almost ran over my legs.

I realize I probably shouldn't have had them out in the road like that, but he didn't have to aim for them. Anyway, it was nice of him to stop for us. He even helped us throw our paraplegic bikes on top of the bus.

If the trains we'd been traveling on were third-class, that bus was fourth. The lady next to me had a goat between her legs and a chicken on her lap. Either that or the grass hadn't worn off yet.

Günter went right to sleep. Instead of waiting for the next uncontrollable attack, I deliberately set out to write a poem for him:

DREAMLOVE

I remember—
  why don't you?
We slept together.
  We embraced.
  We loved.
I remember—
  why don't you?

I decided that I shouldn't give that one to him. He probably didn't want to be reminded of my spy dream. I tried another one:

I will be me.
You will be you.
But let us be
Each other too.

Sounded too much like a greeting card, I thought, or something somebody would write in your high school yearbook. Somebody did write that in my high school yearbook! Charley!

That meant I hadn't just created that little poem. It had popped out of my past. What about the others? Did they pop out of my past too?

I rememberd when Charley wrote that. It was the summer after ninth grade . . . just before he got taken away. He had waited until summer vacation to write in my annual because he didn't want anybody else to read what he had to say. He was that way about a lot of stuff the last couple of years we were together. Secretive. I think it had something to do with our increasingly active sex life. When we were still just fooling around, he was very open about his affection for me—throwing his arms around me, falling on top of me and stuff like that—but he stopped all that when we started really getting down to it.

It was inevitable that we'd start experimenting (if a hand can feel that good, what about a . . . ?). It was at the County Fair, not long after the camping trip. We were in the fun house. We got separated shortly after we went in and I was looking all over the place for him, going down narrow, dark halls with all those laughing and screaming dummies that jump out at you. One of them grabbed me and pulled me back into a dark corner. It unzipped my pants! It was Charley!

"What are you doing?"

"I want to try something," he said.

"In here?"

"Yes, in here."

"What?"

"You'll see."

Of course, I got a boner before he could even get it out of my pants. He dropped to his knees and startled the hell out of me.

"Charley," I whispered, "you can't do that in here. Take that out of your mouth right now. Charley, someone will catch us. I . . . uh . . . oh . . . uh oh . . . I . . . .oh shit!"

"Whataya think?" he asked me.

"I think you're crazy. Did I hurt your ears?"

"No. I mean, how did it feel?"

"How do you think it felt? Jesus."

"Now me," he said.

"No way."

"You better."

"I won't. Not in here, anyway."

"I'll tell your mother about . . ."

"About what?"

". . . everything."

I gagged on it. I told you he was about a year older than I was. And bigger. I mean bigger.

"Shit, that's nothing compared to a man's dick," he told me.

Charley knew what a man's dick looked like because he had a father.

I didn't have a father. Good Ol' Mom told me that Good Ol' Pop was dead, but I didn't necessarily believe it. She's a bigger liar than I am. My guess is that he ran away. If I'd've been him, I would've run away. I did, as a matter of fact. Run away. Regularly.

Besides the usual reasons like spankings and rejection and adventure, the main reason I ran away all the time was that I thought it would keep this one particular dream from coming true. It was a dream I had at least twice a week for almost a year.

I'm about six years old in the dream and I'm with my daddy who is blind. He's dressed in a white suit and is wearing a straw hat. I'm wearing what best can be described as a "cute little outfit." We're inseparable, my daddy and I – always playing together. We play ball and we wrestle on the big bed and go for long walks. Everything. When we're walking, he holds my hand or just puts his hand on the top of my head or holds on to the back of my shirt. I'm his Seeing Eye Dog.

My Daddy and I go to this carnival and it's inside a great big, beautiful building that has giant chandeliers and huge doors you could drive a truck through and rooms as big as a football field.

We go on all the rides and play all the games and then we go to the sideshow with all the freaky stuff and people in it. There's a giant snake and a fat lady and a man with tattoos and something with two heads!

Then, all of a sudden, my daddy and I are standing in this little room all by ourselves. It's dark at first, then all these colored lights flash on and sitting right in front of us is this naked, strange thing that looks like it's half-man and half-woman. My mouth drops open and I stare at it. It's quite fascinating. It has a man's face, but it is so pretty. It has muscled shoulders and arms and the arms reach out to me like it wants me to come to it. I want to go but I just stand there frozen. It has these big tits and I stare at them too. And it has hair on its belly! And it has a little peepee like mine! I stare at it too.

My daddy walks right up to the thing and starts touching it all over. I yell at him to stop! He touches it on the tits and belly and between the legs. I cry and beg him to come away with me. Then he's naked and he starts kissing it all over! I grab one of his arms and try to pull him away from it! I scream as hard as I can, but he won't get off of the thing! He rolls all over it and then the thing splits open right down the middle and swallows up my daddy! I scream even louder! The thing starts lauging louder than I'm screaming . . . so loud that it hurts my ears! The thing reaches out and grabs me by the hand and I can't pull away! It pulls me closer to it—so close that I can feel and smell its breath. I close my eyes as tight as I can and scream as loud as I can. I shake violently. Then I don't feel its arms around me anymore and I open my eyes. It's gone.

I am alone in the room. The lights go out. The walls begin to move away. The room gets bigger and bigger and bigger!

Tap. Tap. Tap. It's my daddy's cane! He's looking for me! I call out to him. Tap, tap, tap. I run toward the sound, but when I get to where the sound was coming from, my daddy isn't there! That thing is there and it's laughing at me and trying to grab me! Taptaptap! I run the other way and the whole thing happens over again. And over again. And again. Until I'm crying so hard that I choke and that wakes me up.

I really was afraid that dream would come true. I thought my daddy would come back and the Mother would have to tell me that he wasn't dead after all. I was afraid he would be blind and would want to take me to the carnival. So, I ran away a lot and the dream didn't come true. This went on for a whole year after Charley and I went to the County Fair. It was the same year my grandpa died. It was the same year Charley got to shave for the first time. It was the same year they put my grandma in a home for old people. It was the same year I got my full crop of pubic hairs ("pubes" as we kids used to call them and then giggle).

Just thinking about that awful dream sent shivers down my spine. Most of my dreams sent shivers down my spine. Why the mixed genders? And why were people represented in duplicate? My halves seemed to be having a hell of a time finding each other in the deep, dark recesses of my mind, creating some bizarre situations.

Still, I had become quite fond of dreaming and somewhat proud of the dream skills I'd developed on my European sojourn—like resuming a dream after it had been interrupted and manipulating the action in a dream when things weren't the way I wanted them to be and creating scenes where I could see what was going on without being a participant. Granted, these were rare instances, but it did comfort me to know that my subconscious didn't always have to be out of control.

Mind you, my affection for the dreams and their occasional submission to control did not keep me from doubting my sanity. *Au contraire!* But then, I thought, as I noticed that the chicken sitting next to me on that bus was staring at me, my conscious mind was just as bizarre as its hidden counterpart and there didn't seem to be much I could do about it anyway. I stared back at the chicken.

The bus didn't get into Casablanca until the next morning. I woke up with a stiff neck and a numb left leg. The goat had eaten my shoelaces. I was relieved that there really was a goat. The woman gave me an egg as payment for damages.

We sold the bikes to a garage owner for next to nothing and went looking for a cheap motel.

There was no such animal in Casablanca. We were able to find one that was moderately priced and that had a vacancy. One vacancy. One bed. I kept my mouth shut, but Günter told the woman we'd take it. I wondered if we were going to have to sleep in shifts in that one bed. I couldn't imagine him ever crawling into the same bed with me again.

We unpacked without saying too much. I thought I'd keep quiet about the bed and just wait to see what happens later.

"We should go find Stacey and her friends," he said.

"I just have to do one thing and I'll be right with you," I told him. I was having another attack.

"I will meet you downstairs," he said and left.

I ran to my knapsack and rifled through it for my journal. When I finally found it, I ripped out a blank page and wrote:

Günter,
> Let's not run
>> from those awful moments
>>> when life gives us
>>>> such a fear!
> Let's jump on them!
>> Beat them up!
>>> Drive them back!
>>>> And fuck'em in the ear!!!
>>>>> —Tad

12.   The Green Connection!

"*Die Rote Mühle ist nicht rote!*" Günter said.

Le Moulin Rouge n'est pas rouge!

¡El Molino Rojo no está rojo!

The Red Mill is not red!

It was green! And it was also not next to the Hotel Claire. And vice versa.

"Where the hell are they?" I asked.

"We can look in a telephone book for the hotel," he suggested.

"Good idea, if we can find one."

"There is a public telephone over there," he said.

We went over there. We got the address of the Hotel Claire. We walked.

"I hope they're still there," I said.

"Yes. We will need to get some money from them," Günter said.

"Hey! We came to see them because they're our friends—not to get money from them!"

"I did not mean to say it that way, but we do not have very much money left."

"We have enough."

"Why do you get so angry with me? You took money from them in Barcelona."

"I didn't take money from them; they just paid for stuff when we went out."

"You think there is a difference?" he said.

"I do. There's the hotel."

The Hotel Claire was, in fact, next door to a little bar called The Red Mill. It was red. The hotel was beige.

Stacey was walking out the front door. She was green and red. Green dress, red hair.

"Trish!" I shouted, on the run.

"Tadpole?!" she shouted, on the run.

We collided.

"Oh my God!" she said, "I don't believe you actually made it to Casablanca! This is wonderful! Oh, you couldn't have come at a better time. Everything is just awful! Hi Günter. Everything is falling apart! Everyone is fighting. No one is even speaking to anyone else. Dierdre thought Biff was trying to make time with me, so she told him to go to hell and she thought I was willing, so she's mad at me too. Biff blames me because I haven't been able to talk any sense into her. Oh! and Mike caught Toby taking some kind of pills that Wally gave him and they had a huge fight! So, of course, I tried to patch it up and now they're both mad at me because they each think I was taking the other one's side and we haven't sold any magazines and Wally stays away all the time because he says we're all too crazy to work with and he says he may fire us all and strand us in Casablanca! Can he do that?"

I almost got my mouth open.

"Oh! And because Dierdre wouldn't sleep with Biff, he had to stay in Mike and Toby's room and they weren't sleeping together and since there was only one bed, which Toby had, Mike and Biff both slept on the floor. Well, Dierdre decided that meant they had slept together and they must have 'done something' as she put it, and she confronted Mike who called her a capital *K* which pissed Biff off and he hit Mike in the eye! Oh Tad, I'm so glad to see you! You too Günter. What are we going to do? Did I leave anything out?"

I was out of breath. I waited for a four-count. The silence was deafening.

"That was remarkable," Günter said.

"Thanks," Stacey said. "Well?"

"Stacey, you can't make these people your whole life you know," I said.

"Look who's talking," she said, indicating Günter and embarrassing me.

"At least I'm holding up. How about some lunch?"

"How will that help?" she wanted to know.

"Well, it will rid me of my hunger pains so that I can think and it will put something in your mouth so I can get a word in edgewise."

"I suppose you thought that was funny," she said.

"Fair?" I said, looking to Günter for his vote.

"Not bad," he voted.

"You're both a laugh a minute. Okay, let's eat. I'm starved," she said, leading the way.

We bought a beef stick, cheese, bread, fruit and wine and had a picnic in a small park not far from the hotel.

We had to go over the list of catastrophies again because Günter and I couldn't remember half of them. We couldn't think of anything that would help, but then we had just started on the jug of wine. Given enough wine, you can always come up with solutions. You may come up with a stupid solution, but you will come up with something.

I did.

I suggested, and got clobbered on the arm, that we lock all six of them in a room, naked, and not let them out until they were all lovey-dovey again.

We compromised. We took Wally off the list, included Günter and me, made clothing optional and added the most important ingredient: Stacey had found a connection for Absinthe!

Absinthe! The green muse! Inspiration to poets! Elixir to artists! Gondola to green-tinted hallucinations! Manna! Ambrosia! Liqueur of the gods! Key to enlightenment! Expander of consciousness! Provender of new awareness! Gateway to dreamland! Illegal – and thus adventurous! The solution! Or, if not, no one would give a rat's ass anyway.

Wally, of all people, had given her the name of someone he knew who, Wally was sure, would be able to get us our Absinthe.

"His name is Hermes Trismegistus," Stacey said.

"Not *the* Hermes Trismegistus?" I asked.

"You know him?" she asked.

"Sort of. The name means Hermes thrice greatest. He was the Greek personification of the Egyptian god Thoth and their own god Hermes."

"Probably not the same one," Stacey jested.

"He was supposedly the one who brought knowledge from the gods to earth," I continued, ignoring her levity, "especially the knowledge of magic, astrology, and alchemy—the search for the philosophers' stone and immortality."

"How do you know so much about him?" she asked.

"We went to school together," I said.

"When do we go to this person?" Günter asked, always the practical one.

"He said any night after eight, so we can do it tonight. Now, tell me about your trip. It must have been exciting. Where are your bicycles?"

We told her about our exciting trip. Günter did most of the talking, which was just fine with me because I wouldn't have known which parts to tell and which not to.

For a person who usually never says more than six words at any given time, Günter turned out to be quite the storyteller (spell that l-i-a-r). I barely recognized the story and I was in it. You would've thought we were the Beau Brummells of Club Med . . . and that was the part about La Linea where we hardly ever saw each other and barely spoke. And Bobadilla! I damned near fell off the blade of grass I was perched on! Quaint little village, he said. Lovely people, he said. Beautiful mountains, he said. Charming inn, he said. Great dreamsuck! I wanted to say but didn't.

I shared some of my poetry with them. Günter even seemed interested, which surprised me. He liked "Afrika." Stacey couldn't believe that I'd sent it to the Mother, but she couldn't believe I'd written it either. I explained how I'd been possessed off and on recently. They both seemed to move away from me when I said that, but I figured it was just my imagination.

The wine made me sleepy, so I headed back to the room for a nap. Stacey and Günter said they wanted to go check out Casablanca's oceanside cliffs and would wake me in time to go after the Absinthe.

As I was crossing the lobby of our moderately-priced-but-still-not-cheap hotel, I heard my name and to my chagrin, Mike came running across the lobby to throw his arms around me and kiss me on the mouth! I wondered why the long lost buddy greeting, but I needn't have been embarrassed about the kiss—the woman at the desk thought we were adorable.

"How'd you know to come here?" I asked him.

"I saw you on the street and followed you."

"Why did you wait till. . .?"

"I thought it might embarrass you if I greeted you like that on the street."

"But the lobby is. . .you're absolutely right! Come on up to the room."

"Only one bed?" he asked as we entered the room.

"I guess so," I said too casually.

"Didn't Günter come with you?"

"Yeah. Where's Toby?"

"I don't know," he said too casually.

"Sit." He sat on the bed. I pulled the chair up next to the bed and straddled it backwards thinking I looked more macho that way. I didn't. "I take it that Stacey was not exaggerating then?"

"You've seen Stacey?"

"Yeah, she and Günter went for a walk. It's great to see you." I knew he was troubled about something because his mustache was disheveled.

"You too," he said and seemed to mean it, so I decided it was time to find out if I was imagining the hostility from him earlier.

"I got the impression in Barcelona that you didn't think too much of me," I said courageously, afraid he was going to confirm it.

"Really?"

"Really. I thought at the time that maybe you were afraid Toby was attracted to me."

"Well it. . ."

"I also wondered if. . .no, I was afraid that you had noticed that I was attracted to you and what I was seeing was repulsion."

"Hm. I. . .uh. . .maybe a little of both. . .but not repulsion, Tad. Definitely not repulsion."

Silence. The kind of silence that lets the imagination stray dangerously toward action that should not be allowed to happen.

"So!" I blurted out, "What's with you and Toby?"

"Nothing."

"Bullshit! What kind of pills was he on?"

"I don't know. Speed. But that wasn't. . .he's been so bitchy lately, about everything. We even fought over the toothpaste this morning."

"How do you fight over toothpaste?"

"I don't squeeze it right, apparently."

"And your sex life?" Busybody.

"Nil. You used to fuck girls didn't you?"

"Yeah."

"So did Toby. Do you miss it?"

"Uh. I don't know. You think Toby misses getting a little pussy now and then?"

"I guess so."

"Did he say so?"

"Not exactly, but he does talk about it. A lot."

"Then give him some."

"I. . .I. . .uh. . ." I embarrassed him.

"You brought it up, Mike."

"I know, but. . ."

"Why not?"

"Well. . . .he's the girl in our. . ."

"What the hell is that supposed to mean?!"

"It means I. . .he. . .it means I fuck him, if you must know."

"What I must know is what makes you think that either one of you is the girl in your relationship? You're two guys! Two boys. Men maybe. Both with the same equipment anyway. And both capable of the same needs!"

"I suck him off," Mike said.

"How generous of you. And is a blow job all you ever want?"

"No."

"Maybe it isn't all Toby wants either. And it wouldn't hurt you to offer."

"But wouldn't he have said something?"

"Not necessarily. He might be afraid you'd reject him. That stops a lot of people from asking for a lot of things. Maybe he'll choose to remain passive all the time or only take the top once a year, but at least you'll both know where you stand. . .lie."

"I don't know. We tried it once when we first got together and it. . .uh. . .it seemed awkward somehow. And we wound up going back to our usual."

"Try it with massage sometime. Ask him to give you a rubdown, with you on your stomach, and then guide him to it slowly with little suggestions. If he. . .no, when he starts to get amorous, beg him to fuck you. Order him if you have to." Now, I said to myself, we're going to have to change the subject or I'm going to attack you myself!

"It might be nice," Mike mused.

"And if you let yourself get carried away, it won't hurt so much."

"I don't worry about the pain," he said weakly.

"You don't?"

"Well. . .a little."

"I do. . .a lot."

"Don't you get used to it?" he asked.

"I don't know."

"Whatayou mean you don't know?!"

"I've never done it."

"Then how the hell do you. . .?!"

"What difference does it make? Is it something you want to happen?"

"Yes."

"So?"

Pause.

"What if he doesn't do it? Or doesn't like it?"

"Then you'll have gotten a free massage. But! if he does like it, you'll have a new alternative for all those times, when you guys get bored trying to think of things to do."

"I'm not sure I'll even be speaking to him to ask for the massage," Mike said, remembering the last few days.

"Your loss."

"No. I will try."

"Don't count on it to solve your problems, but maybe you can open up the communication a little."

"I hope so."

"We've got a little surprise for you all tonight, so try to be at the hotel after eight. Okay?"

"No problem."

"Now I need a nap, so unless you want to take one with me. . .?"
I said jokingly. Ha.

"I'm going."

"Sometimes I wish. . ."

"What?"

"Nothing. See you tonight."

"Yeah."

"Bye."

"Bye."

He understood. I was very proud of me for not trying to get him
into that bed.

I got me into bed. It was one of those sweaty naps. Fitful, with
repeated falling sensations. I was more exhausted when I got up than
I'd been when I went to bed. I was showered and dressed by the time
Günter and Stacey came to get me.

We set out to find the legendary Hermes Trismegistus.

"Where does he live?"

"Come wiz me to ze Casbah," Stacey clowned.

"At night?! Are you crazy?!"

Casbah simply means the native section of any North African city—in
the dictionary, that is. In real life, Casbah means danger! It means drugs
and prostitution and murder and spies and daggers and all that other
great stuff you see in movies. The Casbah in Casablanca made Barcelona's harbor district look like Disneyland.

"Why not?" Stacey asked.

"Because I'm not ready to die!" I sobbed.

"Absinthe!" Günter said, manipulatively.

"Right! In we go guys."

I've never been so scared in my life. I just knew we were signing
our death warrants. Stacey would be kidnaped by white slavers. I'd
be killed or seriously wounded trying to rescue her. Günter would
make a hundred bucks and change on the sale. I had no hopes for
that trip at all.

It was everything it's cracked up to be. Dark, narrow alleyways. Sus-
picious types lurking in the shadows. Strange sounds and smells that

defied recognition. God, it was like Tijuana! I took the point; Stacey was in the middle; Günter was rear guard. The lights were so dim, we could barely make out the street names on the corners of the old, white buildings. Some of the signs were inset into hand-crafted relief sculptures. The place was very beautiful. It would have been terrifically romantic if we had a squad of marines with us.

We found the number. Well, we didn't exactly find the number. We were looking for 14. The door to our left said 12. The door to our right said 16. The door in front of us said 666, but it had to be 14 so we knocked.

No answer.

Knock. Knock.

A man, an especially scuzzy man, ran out of an alley across the street and then up to us. He did something with his mouth that would have been a smile if he had any teeth. Stacey grabbed my arm. Günter asked him what he wanted. The dirty little man reached into his jacket. This is where we eat the afterbirth, I thought. I knew it was going to be a dagger he'd pull out of that jacket. Or dirty postcards. It was a chicken. A dead chicken. A plucked dead chicken. Stacey made a noise. And a very deep impression in my forearm.

"*Va te faire foutre, enculeur de mouches!*" I shouted at him!

He did.

I had been waiting for years for a situation to arise where I could use that. A friend of mine in college taught it to me and I had never gotten to use it. Politely, it means, "Get your butt out of here, bugger!" What it really means is, "Go get fucked, you who fucks flies in the ass!" I loved it. He probably didn't understand a work I said, with my terrible pronunciation, but I said it with a lot of conviction.

Knock. Knock.

The door opened very slowly. I wanted to say that Wally sent us, but it seemed too flip for this situation. Jesus! It was a six-foot ball of hair!

Stacey's mouth fell open, her eyes widened.

"Gesundheit!" she said.

"You've got to be kidding," I said.

"What?" Günter said.

The hair ball flashed extraordinarily white teeth up where the head would've been if it had been a human being. It indicated we should enter its lair. Stacey practically jumped into the room. Günter entered as though it were a normal place. They pulled me in.

"Are you Hermes Trismegistus?" Stacey asked, with her heart all aflutter.

What is wrong with that girl? I asked myself.

The hair spoke:

> "The eagle driven back around the tents,
> Will be chased by other birds around him:
> When the sound of cymbals, trumpets and bells,
> Will restore sense to the senseless woman."

"Oh my God," Stacey said.

"Nostradamus!" I said.

It flashed those white teeth at me. I thought I caught a glimpse of eyes behind the hair a little higher up. I also caught a glimpse of that room! It was a laboratory! He was an alchemist! Stills and burners, vials of different colored powders, mortars with pestle, three furnaces and listen to this bookshelf: Aristotle. Aquinas. Bacon. Albertus Magnus. Taoism. Yoga. Geology. Chemistry. Physics. Atomic Theory. Astronomy. Astrology. Gnostic Legend. Hermetic Theory. Ancient Gods. Nostradamus!

"Who's he?" Stacey asked.

"A heavy prophet," I told her.

> "The bones will be found inside the wells,
> It will be incest committed by the stepmother:
> The state changed, he will seek renown and praise,
> And will have Mars attendant as his star."

"Sounds like a fascinating man," Stacey gurgled. I was about ready to slap her.

"We were told by a friend that you might be able to get us some Absinthe," I said to the hair.

> "O what horrid and sad torment!
> Shall be put to three innocents,

Poison shall be suspected, evil guards shall betray them.
They shall be put to horror by drunken executioners."
"That's the stuff!" I said.

Hermes went to a cupboard and got out a large bottle of green liquid. He handed it to me. I hugged it.

"How much?" Günter asked. I think it was the only thing he said while we were in that room. He was studying Hermes very closely for some reason. Maybe he liked hair.

"The hidden Sun eclipsed by Mercury,
Will be placed only second in the heavens:
Hermes will be made the food of Vulcan,
The Sun will be seen pure, shining and golden."

"He wants gold," I said. Either that or he wanted to burn in hell, but I didn't think I should say that aloud.

"Twenty bucks American," Hermes Trismegistus incarnate said. I knew he could talk like other people.

"Here," Stacey said, reaching into her purse.

"That's too much," I protested.

"I don't mind. It's worth it," she said and handed the money to Hermes. I was gonna have to have a talk with her later about her taste in men.

Hermes showed us to the door. He shook hands with Günter first, then me. It was the same handshake the Good Samaritan had given me! Is this some kind of brotherhood? I wondered. I felt warm. And eerie. Sincere. Hermes kissed Stacey. . .or rather he brushed hair up against her cheek—lips could never find their way out of that heavy beard.

The door closed behind us.

I just stood there being warm. Stacey just stood there being agog. Günter put me on one arm and Stacey on the other and led us back to the Hotel Claire.

13. Drip. Drip. Drip. Sip. Sip. Sip.

The others were waiting for us in Stacey and Dee's room. They were waiting in silence, having taken up positions as far apart as was possible in the confines of the twin-bedded, single-sinked and spartanly decorated room.

"Took you long enough," Biff greeted us.

"This better be worth it," Dierdre overlapped.

"Hi guys," Mikey said. At last, a friendly voice.

"Well! If it isn't Dear Abby!" Tody lashed.

Uh oh.

"Hey, don't put it off on him," Mike defended me.

"What?" Dierdre wanted to know.

"Who? Mr. Expert on seduction techniques?" Toby said.

"You mean she's not the only one?" Dierdre attacked, glaring at Stacey.

"Don't start on me, Dierdre," Stacey joined the mêlée. "If I was going to seduce anyone around here, it sure as hell wouldn't be Biffff!"

"Thanks a lot, Stace," Biff said.

"Oh that's right, you only go for married men, don't you?" Dierdre said.

Günter was able to grab Stacey midway into her lunge toward Dierdre's pert, uniform breasts.

"I think they have all gone crazy," Günter said as he hauled Stacey off to a neutral corner.

"No," Toby started in again. "It's just that some people can't keep their noses out of other people's business."

"It would seem that there has been very much of that going on here." Günter the Rational said.

"It was fine until Miss-Advice-to-the-Lovelorn arrived." Toby again.

"Oh sure, Toby! Everything was just fine!" Stacey yelled. "We've only been at each other's throats night and day since we left Barcelona!"

"Some. . .yeah," Toby was willing to admit.

"Some?!!" we all screamed.

"I think I've been pretty calm through it all. . .until she got here." He meant me, Dear Abby.

"Calm, did you say?" Mike asked. "Is that why you started wetting the bed again?"

Dead silence. Total. Throat-clearing group embarrassment. A general plea filled the room, vibes in unison wishing someone or something would get us out of this. We don't want to do this anymore, but we don't know how to stop! We seemed to be screaming silently.

Tad to the rescue.

I opened the bottle of Absinthe. Licorice burst out into the room! Relief burst out into the room!

"Licorice whip!" someone said.

"Whip me! Whip me!" Toby squealed.

"Down boy, you haven't even tasted it yet," Mike said, winking at me.

"What is it?" Dierdre asked.

"Absinthe," Stacey said.

"Green Magic!" I said.

"Where did you get it?" Biff asked.

"You wouldn't believe it," I said.

"From a wonderful and charming man by the name of Hermes Trismegistus," Stacey drooled.

"Not *the* Hermes Trismegistus?" Mike asked.

"Tad already told me about the one who was some-thingoranother with the Greeks," Stacey pouted.

"No, no! A big guy! With hair for days!" Toby said, jumping up and down. Mike touched him on the arm to settle him down.

"You do know him!" Stacey said.

"He introduced us!" Mike said.

"At the Russian River," Toby added.

"*The* Russian River?" I asked.

"Yeah, near San Francisco," Mike said.

"I went to the Russian River once," I said, but was totally ignored.

"We were both staying at one of the gay resorts there," Mike continued, "but hadn't met each other yet. Hermes. . ."

"I got sick," I said.

". . .was telling fortunes in the village there. . ." Toby continued for Mike.

"And never got to do anything," I said.

". . .and we wound up sitting in his waiting room together," Mike continued for Toby.

"It felt like a flu," I said.

"Been together ever since," Toby added.

"Off and on," Mike added, winking at me.

"Although it might've been allergies," I said.

"What a small and wonderful world we live in," Stacey said in her best Pollyanna manner.

"And it rained the whole time I was there," I told myself.

"What did you think of him?" Toby asked.

"Wild," Günter said.

"Weird!" I said, giving up on my story.

"Wonderful!" Stacey said.

"He is, isn't he?" MikenToby said.

"Are we ready to try this?" I asked.

"Yeah! I'll get the glasses," Toby offered.

"Go ahead, but we do have to prepare it first," I told them. I had studied up on the proper method of consuming Absinthe. The best way is called an Absinthe Drip, but that requires special glasses from France. We faked it. We got a hot water bottle with one of those long tubes on it and filled it with crused ice (Mike ran down to the lobby) and sugar cubes (Toby raided Wally's stash) and purified water (Biff went to a neighborhood market for bottled).

"What you do is put a shot of Absinthe into the glass." I did. "Then you drip the sugar water very slowly into the liqueur." I did. "First, it turns milky." It did. "Then cloudy." It did. "And finally opalescent!" Voilá!

"Sip. Sip. Sip," I warned them. "This pretty green booze runs 136 proof—that's 68 per cent alcohol."

Absinthe has been banned throughout most of the civilized world because the wormwood (an herb) in it supposedly causes hallucinations (I was hoping so!) and has been rumored to cause insanity and even death. Most experts now feel that it wasn't the wormwood at all, just too much alcohol in one place at one time. The average liquor is only 40 per cent alcohol compared to Absinthe's 68 per cent. That is called brain damage.

We did go slowly. I think we were all a little frightened of that mythological liquid.

MikenToby were the first to make the happy reunion physical. They were all over each other—apologizing and apetting. Nobody cared. It was just affectionate stuff.

Dierdre and Biff were bound together before we finished the first round of drinks. They were considerably less demonstrative, but a lot more nauseating.

Drip. Drip. Drip.

Sip. Sip. Sip.

> "A silly young fairy named Bloom
> Took a lesbian up to his room
>> And they argued a lot
>> About who would do what,
> And how, and with which, and to whom," Toby said.

I fell off my chair.

Sip. Sip. Sip.

"You know what I think?" Dierdre slurred from the floor where she was lying with her head in Biff's lap, her face turned half into his crotch.

"Don't talk with your mouth full, Deedee!" Biff quipped and started howling.

"Biff!" we all said.

Deedee bit Biff!

Sip. Sip. Sip.

"My neck is still stiff from sleeping on that bus last night," I complained.

"What you need is a good face-fucking!" Mike said.

"Mike!" Stacey scolded.

"Sorry," Mike apologized.

"Besides," she went on, "that's probably what caused it in the first place!"

"Stacey!" we all shouted.

Everybody, except me, looked at Günter.

"I am not telling," he said.

The blush, the telltale burning, began at the top of both my ears and spread rapidly over my whole body. Fingers were being pointed at me. The laughter was mocking. I pulled my sweater over my head until I could tell by the noise that they were all rolling on the floor and, thus, not looking at me anymore. I pulled the sweater back down.

Günter smiled at me.

Sip. Sip. Sip.

Stacey got out her flute and began to play. Once in a while, someone threw in a lyric or two. Once or twice the lyric actually went with the song she was playing. Mike got his guitar from his room and joined her. We were all just sort of sprawled out on the floor. Stacey ran out of wind, so Mike soloed for a while. Toby worked his way around behind Mike and began to massage his neck and shoulders. I let out a single, voiceless, laugh. Toby giggled. Mike closed his eyes, well on his way to ecstasy. Dee and Bee were intertwined. And I wound up with Stacey at my side and Günter facing me, knee to knee.

Mike's soft guitar was lulling me to sleep. I closed my eyes. I felt something moving up my leg and into my crotch. I opened my eyes. It was Günter's foot! Now shoeless. I rested my hand on his foot and closed my eyes again. I felt something coming around my side, across my belly and down into my crotch. I opened my eyes. It was Stacey's hand!

Stacey's hand was not at all pleased to meet up with Günter's foot in my crotch. In fact, Stacey's hand was so embarrassed that it got flustered. Then angry. Then bitchy!

"Sorry! I didn't know that spot was taken," she said, much too loud.

"Stacey, come on," I tried.

"No, please, don't pay any attention to me. I wouldn't want to keep anyone from having a gay old time, as they used to say."

"What's with her?" Toby asked.

"Her is just fine, thank you!"

"Stacey, please," I tried again, "you accused Dierdre of being a capital *K* and now you're being one."

"She what?!" Dee asked.

"Well you're a capital *P.H.*" Stacey screamed!

"A what?"

"*P.H.*! Phhhhaggot!!!" she spit and then started to cry. "Why do you all have to be faggots?"

"I'm not," Biff announced proudly.

Dierdre got a firm grip on Biff's balls and also announced proudly: "You're going to be a eunuch if you don't shut up, lover boy!" Well, that's approximately what she said. There were a few too many syllables and a lot of extra 'R's in there, but that's what she meant.

I pulled Stacey to me and put my arm around her. I'm not sure, but I think she wiped her nose on my sweater.

"Next time, make reservations. Okay?" I joked.

She hit me in the stomach.

"Can I have some more green magic?" she asked.

"Let's all have some more green magic!" I said.

Drip. Drip. Drip.

Sip. Sip. Sip.

"And let's play a game," I said.

"Your games are too strange," Biff said.

"You'll like this one," I told him, "It's called Murder Conspiracy. We all conspire to kill somebody!"

"Wally!!" they all shouted! Even Günter who still hadn't met Wally.

"Okay, Wally it is. When?"

"Now!"

"He's not here now. It will have to be later tonight."

"It has to be done before morning."

"How?"

"Stab him!"

"With a dildo!"

"Shoot him!"

"With a dildo!"

"Hang him!"

"By the balls!"

"Poison him!"

"With a suppository!"

"Drown him!"

"In shit!"

I'd never seen such enthusiastic players before. We voted on death by strangulation.

"Who does it?"

"I will!" they all shouted!

Richard Dawson would kill to get this bunch on "Family Feud."

The door opened. Mike forgot to relock it when he went to get his guitar. It was Wally!

"Just dropped by to pick up something. You need anything Toby?" Wally said.

"He's got everything he needs, thank you," Mike said.

"Okay, don't jump on my back. Sounds like a party in here." Wally was looking much better. His clothes were pressed. His hair was combed. He was clean shaven. And I ventured to guess that his taste in women had improved greatly, judging by the aroma of expensive perfume wafting in from the young woman whose leg I could see out in the hall.

"A private party," Stacey said.

"Ah come on, you're not gonna share with your Uncle Walter? Oh! What is that I see? I do believe the children have latched onto some elixir? Come to papa, you wonderful green mindfuck."

He took my glass and downed it.

"Oops!" he said, "I think you guys got taken. Old Hermes gotya! What you have here, my young friends, is a little anisette with a lot of grain alcohol."

"You're kidding! Please!" I moaned.

"Nope. It's big business down here. They sell gallons of this shit to the tourists. And make a bundle doing it. Tell you what, I'll go see that crook tomorrow and get you some of the real thing. You'll love it. Gotta run now. Hot date! Bye."

And out he went.

"Come on," Biff said. "Let's kill him now."

"Not if he's going to get us the real stuff!" I said.

Günter leaned over to me and whispered in my ear, "Want to have another spy dream?"

"We have to leave now!" I announced.

14. Follow That Dream!

I couldn't believe it. I thought I must've been dreaming. Or that Wally was wrong and it really was Absinthe and this was a hallucination. Nope. There I was walking down the street with Günter and we were on our way back to our hotel room to. . .uh. . .have an awake wet dream.

"Do you have to skip?" he asked me.

"Oh. Sorry." How embarrassing.

But I didn't really care. I couldn't care about anything at that moment. I wasn't skipping, I was soaring. In two blocks, I would be alone with him in that room. In one block, we'd be in bed together. Just around the corner, we'd get naked and. . . .

Goddamnmotherfuckingcocksuckingsonofabitch!!!!

Our hotel was surrounded by police! Our hotel was barricaded! Our hotel was unattainable!

There had to be a hundred police out there! And a thousand spectators! It took seventeen conversations in three languages to get six tidbits of information. All anyone knew was that a man and a transvestite were busted trying to make a large drug buy and the man had taken hostages. And the police thought it was going to take all night to get them out of there!

I sat down on the curb and cried.

"Let's go for a walk," Günter said.

It was a beautiful, moonlit night. I could have really enjoyed it if I hadn't been so goddamn pissed off!

I think we walked for an hour. Somewhere along the way he put his arm around my shoulder and pulled my arm around his waist. Then I wasn't angry anymore.

Then we were standing silently, arm in arm, looking out into nothingness. I could see the moon's relfection in the water off in the distance.

"The water seems so far away," I said.

"That is because we are so high," he said.

"Oh," I said, thinking he meant high on booze. "What's that noise?"

"Ocean waves," he told me.

"Where's it coming from?"

"Down there."

"Where?"

"There."

Holy shit! We were standing right at the edge of a cliff a hundred feet above the water! Straight down!! I got dizzy. Günter steadied me.

He kissed me. I felt strange kissing someone who was taller than I am. Somehow inferior. Somehow passive. Somehow dominated. I inched up onto a flat rock that was next to my left foot. I felt more comfortable. Somehow equal. I kissed him.

"Do you want to make love?" he asked me.

"Here?!"

"Yes."

"I can't even breathe! How'm I gonna make love?!"

"Try," he said, removing his sweater.

Oh god.

I'm not going to tell you what happened. It's too embarrassing. Oh what the hell! I fainted. And it wasn't from the sight of his naked body glistening in the moonlight. Or because I was freezing out there, nude, on that high cliff. I fainted because when he knelt and put his arms around my hips, I looked down at the water instead of at him and fell dead away on top of him. And I don't know if he continued or not because I was unconscious for some time.

If karma exists, I must have done something really terrible at one time or another. Our love affair was not made in heaven, that's for goddamn sure!

"*Guten Morgen*," Günter said.

I was in bed. Naked.

"Was that a dream?" I asked.

"No," he answered.

"Is this our hotel room?"

"Yes. The man got away from the police. Would you like some coffee?"

"Yes. You said '*Guten Morgen*.' Does that mean it's morning?" I asked.

"Yes. See?" He pointed to the window which was filled with obvious daylight.

"Where did you get coffee?"

"Around the corner."

Why is he being so nice to me? I wondered. I didn't feel sore anywhere.

"Did you carry me back here?" I asked. He lit a cigarette and handed it to me.

"Wally gave us a lift."

"Wally?"

"Yes. After I finally got your clothes back on you, I started carrying you. Then Wally came by in a car and brought us back here. There's more coffee if you want some."

I nodded. He poured it for me and then sat on the bed next to me.

"I liked the poem you wrote for me," he said.

"What poem?"

"About fear."

"Oh. yeah. Thanks." I was getting very confused. The situation was a lot easier to deal with in my fantasies, in my dreams and under the influence of alcohol than it was in real life. . .in broad daylight.

He put his hand on my chest. My heart tried to pound its way out of its cage. Breathing became impossible.

What if he wants to have intercourse anally? I thought. With my anally? I'd never done that before. I was a virgin!

Günter was rubbing something on my chest. Günter was also naked! When did he do that? And what is that stuff he's rubbing on me?

"What is that?"

"Oil."

"What kind of oil?"

"I don't know."

"Where'd you get it?"

"Hermes."

"Hermes?" Why am I having to drag all this out of him?

"He gave it to me when we shook hands. See, it says 'Rub gently on Tad's body and it will drive him crazy.'"

"Let me see that!"

"No. It says 'Rub gently on skin for sensuous pleasure. May also be used as a lubricant.'"

Uh oh.

The rubbing had progressed to my belly.

"Look, Tad *hat einen Steifen*," Günter said.

"*Einen* what?"

"*Einen Ständer.*"

"Oh. Yeah." Hard as a rock. Peeking out of the covers.

So did Günter. Have *einen Steif Ständer*.

We didn't fuck. What we did was rub that oil on each other. All over. And under. And in between. And then lick it off. Completely. Twice. Each.

Ever have sore tongue muscles? It's weird.

It took all day. And most of the night.

I was angry with Hermes for cheating us on the Absinthe, but I would be eternally grateful to him for his magic oil.

"Why did it take so long for this to happen?" I asked Günter. We were sitting naked on the window ledge, looking at the city lights.

"I am not sure. I think it was because I did not trust you enough."

"Trust me how?"

"To not. . .I do not know."

I got cigarettes for us and then stood leaning against him.

"I would like to understand," I told him.

"People always want to buy me. I thought you wanted to buy me also."

"Not on my budget."

"That is not. . ."

"I know. I'm sorry. I'm afraid you're right though. If I would've had any money, I probably would've tried to buy you. Maybe letting Stacey and the others pay for both of us was doing just that."

"What do you mean?" he asked.

"I mean that I invited you to go along with us in Barcelona because I knew that they would pay for everything. I guess I hoped you'd be grateful. I also remember that I kept handing you cigarettes faster than you could smoke them. And I also kept passing the wine bottle to you that night after *La Guitarra*, even when it hadn't been around to the others yet. I don't blame you for not trusting me. I was trying to buy you. I don't deserve. . . ."

He stuck his tongue in my mouth to shut me up.

I slept like a baby that night, nestled in his arms. Morning felt terrific! I reached for the bottle of oil. It was empty!

Günter rolled on top of me. I closed my eyes. (Have you ever watched a cat hesitating just outside some new, dark adventure? You can tell that it's scared to death, but that it's dying to do whatever it is. Curious as hell, but tentative—that's how I felt at that moment.) Günter was nibbling my neck. I opened my eyes, unfortunately letting out one of those little personal and very private moans that we save for moments of ecstasy. I say unfortunate because when I opened my eyes, I was looking right into Stacey's eyes!

"Stacey!" I screamed in poor Günter's ear.

"Hi," she said, calmly.

"Hello," Günter said, calmly.

I wasn't calm at all! "What the hell are you doing in here?!" I tried to grab the covers, but they were stuck under Günter's legs and he wasn't moving. "Move!" I yelled! He did. Just slightly. His tan line was still exposed to the world. How can they be so calm? I'm lying in bed naked. There is a naked may lying on top of me. There is a woman friend standing right there next to the bed. This is not time for calm. This is time for hysteria!

"Your door wasn't locked," she said.

"I don't care! You could've knocked and waited for someone, anyone, to say 'Come in!'" I pulled the covers so hard that they came up over my head and thus exposed my lower half—the half with the *Ständer*! I gave up. I jumped out of bed to find my pants.

Günter pulled the sheet up to his tan line and settled back on the bed, amused by it all.

"It's important!" Stacey insisted.

"What's important?" I demanded.

"Wally."

"What about Wally?!"

"He's disappeared!"

15. Beach Blanket Banana!

"I hope your spies did not get him," Günter joked sarcastically in response to Stacey's suggestion that Wally might have been kidnaped.

"Your what?" she asked.

"Ignore him," I said and tried the door again.

Knock. Knock.

No answer.

We were back at 14 *Rue de la Decadence*. The residence of one Hermes Trismegistus. Wally had said he would be seeing Hermes. We hoped he would know what happened to Wally.

Günter pounded on the door. It opened.

The room was empty! Totally bare! Furniture, lab equipment, furnaces, books, everything! Gone! How do you move that much shit in one day?

There was an envelope nailed to the back of the door. Stacey opened it and read:

> "The captive escaped through great danger,
> His fortune greatly changed in a short time,
> The people shall be trapped in the palace,
> And by good omen, the city besieged."

"Tad?" Stacey asked.

"Wally's flown the coop," I guessed.

"Why would he do that?" she wondered.

"My guess is that Wally was the fellow who got busted for drugs the other night in our hotel and then took hostages. He apparently got away."

"And he must have taken the money with him," Günter added, reading the second line.

"What about the last two lines?" asked Stacey.

"I hope it doesn't mean we're going to get stuck in Casablanca."

"You may not be, but if Wally is gone, then the rest of us are," she reminded me.

"Oh yeah."

We returned to the Hotel Claire to share our knowledge with the others. Divided emotions: delight over the disappearance; disappointment over the disassociation.

Stacey put in a call to the company offices in Amsterdam. Well, Stacey put in the call, but Günter had to do the talking because the Regional Circulation Manager only spoke German. He said to call again the next day for instructions.

We all (Stacey, MikenToby, Dierdre, Biff, Günter and I) went to the beach. As you may recall, Casablanca has cliffs overlooking its little part of the ocean, so we had to go north of the city to find a beach suitable for recreation. We took a bus.

"A thousand bottles of beer on the wall. . ." MikenToby began to sing.

"No!" I cried. "It's not that far!" I didn't know how far it was—I just knew I wouldn't survive a thousand choruses of that song. They did John Jacob Jenkelheimer Schmidt instead. Günter sang in German. Biff faked it. Dierdre did little cheerleader things without standing. And without pom-poms.

Stacy and I talked.

"Cheer up," I said. "The company'll send you some tickets or something."

"I was thinking about Hermes."

"He'll survive."

"That isn't what I meant."

"Stacey, you can't fall for a guy like that."

"You should talk."

"It's different."

"How?"

"Well, uh. . ."

"Exactly."

"Give me a chance, willya?" I said. "Hermes is a gypsy, a fortune teller, a would-be alchemist! And he's probably mixed up in Wally's drug business. Besides, he's all hair."

"I know. Like a great big Teddy Bear."

O Nostalgia! O Memories! O Teddy Bears!

"We're too old for Teddy Bears," I said.

"We?"

"I meant you."

"I'm not too old," she assured me.

"The cops are probably after him."

"I don't care."

"He probably has three wives already."

"I can be number four."

"He's gone!"

She looked at me as though I'd just strangled her puppy with my bare hands. Hate & Hurt, Inc. With one of those single tears that just hangs there in the corner of the eye, driving you crazy, until it finally lets go and plummets down the cheek. Instant guilt for me.

"I agree there was, is, something very special about him," I told her. And meant it.

Instant forgiveness from her.

I'm not sure why I started in on her again. It just somehow felt unfinished.

"Stacey, I. . .uh. . .you know, actually I envy you a little. . .your affairs, I mean."

"For God's sake, why? They're usually awful."

"You know, never having to make a commitment."

"That's not why I. . ."

"Oh?"

"I told you. . .it all goes back to my father."

"You only see older men then?"

"No, I. . ." was followed by a moment of thoughtful silence.

"Look at what you do. Married men are safe. Hermes would've been safe—you have to know he never would've settled into a permanent relationship. Then there's your attraction to, or if you like, your inclination to be with gay men."

"Are you calling me a fag hag?"

"Mike. Toby. Günter. Me. Others maybe?"

"A couple, I guess, but. . ."

"And that nursery school you. . ."

"Preschool," she tried to correct me.

"That nursery school where you baby-sit other people's kids—not to demean what you or other people do there, if that's the kind of teaching you want to do."

"Not really."

"Then change it."

"But it still must have something to do with the way my father treated me."

"So what? The most important thing to determine is whether or not what you are doing is a problem. If it isn't, then who the hell cares?"

"It's a problem."

"Okay. Then you have to work at solving said problem. . .consciously, deliberately. You just stop doing it. It's called discipline."

"But. . ."

"Then, if you aren't able to conquer it with your own determination, you go find help."

"I don't know if I can conquer it on my own."

"Then?"

"I know."

She scooted over to me and put her head on my shoulder. We cuddled the rest of the way to the beach.

There was some kind of an L-shaped inlet between the road where we got off the bus and the beach where we wanted to go and that meant a long walk. We took the short cut. Over a train trestle. Biff had to drag Dierdre. We told her a little danger was good for the circulation, but she didn't believe us. Danger? There hadn't been a train on those rusty tracks in ten years.

As we got over the water, Günter started taking off his clothes.
"What are you doing?" I asked him.
"Going for a swim," he said.
"Here?"
"Yes."
"You're going to dive off this bridge?"
"Yes."
"But you don't know how deep the water is!"
"It is deep enough."
"I won't let you dive from here. It's too dangerous!" I carried on.
"You do not tell me what to do," he said and handed me his clothes.
He was wearing those spiffy European combination underpants and
swimwear. Red. The stupid sonofabitch!

He climbed up on the railing, hesitated for a second, then dove.
I closed my eyes. The others ran over to the railing to look down at
the poor crumpled body of my. . .whatever he was to me.

Cheers! I opened my eyes. I was pissed as hell. And I stayed pissed
at him all day.

They all ran to the end of the trestle and then down to where he
was coming out of the water. I walked.

MikenToby (as Frankie Avalon and Annette Funicello, respectively)
were the first to reach the sand. They spread out our blankets near
one of the fire rings that dotted the beach for miles in either direction.
And all the pits had firewood in them. How civilized, I thought.

We all stripped. The girls straightened their straps. The boys tucked
the dicks down. Except Mike. He tucked his up. (There's a lot of men
wearing their penises up instead of down lately. Especially in bikinis.)
I was wearing baggy boxer trunks. So was Biff. MikenToby wore bikinis. So did Stacey and Dierdre. You've seen Günter's.

A Sandcastle Contest! MikenToby and I were on one team; Stacey,
Biff and Dierdre on the other. Günter said he wanted to do something
alone and surprise us. I kept my mouth shut on that line. . .with great
difficulty.

"What's wrong with you?" Mike asked me as we began work on

our castle. Apparently my face was on my sleeve again, or whatever that saying is.

"He scared the hell out of me. That's what's the matter."

"He knew what he was doing," Toby joined in.

"He may have. I did not."

"It's his body to bruise if he wants to." That piece of wisdom was from Toby.

"But I asked him not to."

"And you think he should've stopped because you were afraid?" Mike asked.

"Yeah."

"Not reasonable," Toby said.

"I didn't say it was reasonable," I argued.

"You have to let other people live their own lives," Mike said, "even when you *think* you love them."

I smashed one of his spires.

He stuffed a handful of sand down my trunks.

"You tried to stop Toby from taking pills. Isn't that the same thing?" I asked Mike.

"I . . . uh . . ." Mike stammered.

"He did that for us, not just for himself. It's not the same," Toby defended.

"How the hell do you tell the difference?" I wanted to know, desperately.

"You just know."

Terrific. I can't wait.

"Tad," Toby went on, "you were just being protective and possessive with Günter. He was in no real danger and you know it. Most people don't want to be protected or possessed. They just want to be loved. Loved for themselves. Do you want Günter to tell you what to do?"

"I might."

"No you don't. Not the important things anyway. Worry about protecting your relationship after you really have one—after you know you're both in love."

"With each other," Mike added.

"How do you know? Never mind. 'You just do!' "

"You do!"

"But I feel like I love him now."

"And do you also feel he loves you?"

"No."

"See?"

"I see, said the blind man."

As I helped Mike rebuild his spire (the one I had demolished), a man and woman walked up to Toby and asked him to take their picture. They were dressed in matching thongs, pants, flowered shirts, baseball caps, and bellies. They were, of course, Americans.

"Be sure to get our hats in the picture," the woman said.

"No problem," Toby said pleasantly.

"And those two trees back there," she added.

"You got it lady," Toby said agreeingly.

"Look at the camera dear," she told her husband.

"Yes dear," the husband said. He had been looking at Dierdre's tits.

"Ready?" asked Toby amicably.

"Can you show that train bridge too?" she asked.

"Leave him alone," the husband said, looking at Dierdre's tits again, admiring their uniformity.

"Would you like me to show your husband's hard-on, too?" Toby asked vengefully.

I don't remember if she answered. The question scrambled her brains. His, too. They were gone in a huff.

"Tad, as long as we're being honest today," Toby said, "I, uh, think I should apologize."

"Forget it."

"No," Mike said.

"Right," Toby continued. "I was obnoxious. You were trying to help and I got bitchy. I'm sorry."

"You're forgiven."

"The truth is Mike and I do need to communicate with each other more openly and more often . . ."

"Not to mention massage," Mike mentioned.

I couldn't believe it! Toby actually blushed!

"Oops," Mike apologized indirectly, then said to me, "I think I owe you an apology, too,"

"What for?"

"I think I led you to believe our squabbles were Toby's fault and, uh, I just wanted you to know I'm as much to blame as he is. I've been just as nasty on this trip as he has and you might as well know, too, that the reason I got so mad at him over the pills was we'd promised each other before we left home we would both give them up. I was using them even more than he was. Shit, he hardly used them at all. I guess I was afraid that if he fell, I would fall even harder."

"But it's okay now," Toby said.

"Good!" I said, half-wishing we could change the subject.

"We've decided to go back home," Toby continued, "as soon as we figure out how."

"Going to open your flower shop? Or was it antiques?"

"We . . ." Toby began.

"We're moving to San Francisco," Mike finished.

"I thought we were going to discuss this some more," Toby said.

"We did discuss it. You said you wanted to."

"I know, but . . ."

"But what?"

"Your mom . . ."

"She'll get over it. It was all mother's idea in the first place," Mike explained. "She thought it'd be good for us to settle down. She was even going to put up the money . . . which is why we were trying to get our own money together—I didn't particularly want her in on it."

"But you love your mother! Everybody loves your mother!" Toby said.

"Yeah I love her, but I don't want to live with her or be in business with her. She'd be there every day helping out, as she would put it."

"But . . ." Toby whined.

"Toby! Enough" Mike said.

Tension.

I stuffed sand down the back of Mike's bikini. He came after me and when he caught me, we came within inches of falling on top of our creation. Toby played the brave knight and protected the castle from our onslaught, knocking all three of us on our butts in the sand. We ran into the water to rinse off, then went to see how the others were doing.

We held the judging for the best sandcastle.

Our castle had fifteen towers, six walls, a moat-and-a-half and a hot tub. Stacy, Biff and Dierdre only had eight puny towers, four shabby walls and a shallow moat. No hot tub. We were a cinch to win . . . until we saw Günter's surprise. It was a relief sculpture! Of Beethoven! It was spectacular! It looked just like him . . . or the little busts you always see of him. You could see the strands of hair on his head. And facial muscles. And nostrils. It was impressive. It was unanimous—he got the grand prize!

Four joints. But he had to share them.

We smoked two of them right away.

Volleyball was disastrous. We were lousy players. There was no net anyway. No ball either. My team lost. I still don't know how we lost. We had four against their three.

Dinner was a great success. Shish kebob. Bought assembled but un-cooked from a 185-year-old woman in a pony cart. Burnt to a crisp on a huge bonfire.

"It's like this skewered meat . . ." Stacey began.

"Look out!" I warned. "It's a food analogy!"

"You got 'em too?" Mike asked me.

"Bananas and soup so far," I told him.

"You're lucky," Toby continued for Mike. "We've had radishes, straw-berry shortcake, pork chops, raw liver, apples, Chicken Tetrazzini and corn fritters."

"And chocolate-covered bees," Mike added.

"Yech," I yeched.

"You think you're all so funny," Stacey pouted. "Just for that I'm not going to tell you about the skewered meat."

Cheers! Practically a standing ovation.

We passed the other two joints around.

Dessert was also a success. Marshmallows. Bought from the 185-year-old woman on the pony cart. Burnt to a crisp on the coals of the former bonfire.

"Mine's too burnt," Dierdre whined.

"Eat it anyway," Biff grumbled.

"Give it to Mikey," Toby said. "He'll eat anything."

"Hymen!" I cried.

"I married you didn't I?" Mike retorted.

"Hymen!" I tried again.

"Tad, remember what happened to the little boy who cried Hymen too often," Toby warned me.

"Yeah!" Mike added. "Everything isn't a Hymen."

"And vice versa, the former virgin said," I could not resist saying.

"H.Y.M.E.N.!!!" the whole damned bunch screamed!

"I'm not eligible!" I declared confidently.

"We can fix that," Mike said taking the portable cassette and earphones out of his bag.

He and Toby stood and walked around the fire to me.

"It is with great pleasure . . ." Toby began.

". . . and overwhelming pride . . ." Mike continued.

". . . that we bestow on you . . ."

". . . Tadpole Prescott . . ."

". . . the great . . ."

". . . and beneficent . . ."

"Huh?"

"And whatever . . ."

". . . Grand Honor of . . ."

". . . the Hymen!"

They placed the earphones on my head and started the tape: *Henny Youngman Meets Elsie Noosebaum!*

It was wonderful! I laughed hysterically all the way through it! They were so pissed at me they never offered me the honor again! Thank god!

We all kind of just stretched out around the fire. Biff threw on some more wood and cuddled with Dierdre. Mike plucked and Stacey blew. Guitar and flute, respectively.

Günter came over and sat next to me. I hadn't spoken to him since our trestle tiff.

"You scared me," I said.

"I am sorry," he said.

"Promise me you won't do anything like that again."

"No."

"No?"

"I cannot promise you that."

"You have to."

"I do not have to do anything."

"Yeah."

"I do not understand you."

"Me neither."

"Why not just let things happen?" he asked.

"Meaning what?"

"You try too hard. You think about everything too much. You . . ."

"I get the picture!" I was feeling weak and sick to my stomach. I could feel the end coming.

"No you do not. Stop planning everything and maybe, just maybe, it will happen the way you want it to."

"Do you really think it will?"

"That is the point. I do not know. I cannot know. And neither can you. So relax. Okay?"

"Okay, I guess," I guessed.

"Come on."

"Where?"

"Swimming."

"Now?"

"Now."

We ran to the water. He took off his spiffy European combination underpants and swimwear and threw them on the sand. He ordered me to take my trunks off. I did. (See? I did want him to tell me what to do.)

The water was warm. I'd forgotten how good it felt to swim naked.

Günter swam over to me and put his arms around me. I looked toward the beach to see if the others were watching us. He dunked me.

I got away from him and checked the beach again. Everyone was watching us! Great!

Why did the moron swim on his back in the ocean? Because he didn't want the fish to get his worm!

Why did Tadpole swim on his stomach in the ocean? Because Günter was underwater, playing fish!

I remembered Stacey's admonition about the importance of getting down to the banana! Günter was.

Günter Günter boe Bünter!

Banana fana foe Fünter!

Fee fie moe Münter!

Günter!!!!!!!!!!!!!

SING IT SHIRLEY!

16. Put That In Your Fez and Smoke It!

"For God's sake! Take it out!"

"Not yet!"

"It hurts, Toby."

"I know, but it won't take long."

"It's burning the hell out of me!" Mike cried.

"You're the one who wanted this!"

"I know."

"Then stop crying and take it like a man!"

I laughed. It was the kind of thing I'd rather watch than do.

"Don't laugh. You're next," Toby threatened me.

"No way!"

"Don't squirm or it'll come out."

"Did you have to put it in so far?"

"Yes!"

"Well, can't you do it any faster?"

"No!"

"Try!"

"Just shut up!"

Toby pulled out suddenly. Mike groaned with relief.

"Thank God it's over," Mike sighed.

"Oh no it's not."

"Now what?"

"Now I've got to work the earring in before the hole starts to close."

We'd been waiting for over an hour for Stacey and Günter to return from phoning Amsterdam. I thought that having your ear pierced was a little radical just to pass the time away, but Mike had insisted.

Biff and Dierdre had been in and out of the room three times asking if Stacey was back and arguing about which one of them got to wear the navy blue crew neck cashmere sweater that day. When they came back the fourth time, Biff was wearing the sweater. It was eighty-five degrees outside at ten ayem.

Stacey and Günter finally arrived. Money was being wired at that very moment and the group was ordered back to Barcelona to await instructions.

"I can't handle another one of our good-byes," Stacey said as the bus pulled into the depot.

Stacey had asked me to go back to Barcelona with them, but Günter and I decided to hitchhike inland to the ancient city of Fez. Camel country.

"If I don't catch up with you in Barcelona, I promise I'll come straight to Vancouver when I get back to the Americas," I told her.

"If any of us ever get back, you mean."

"We will."

"Please come."

"I can't."

She turned her back to me and got on the bus.

Bye Tadpole, I could feel her thinking.

Bye Trish, I could feel me thinking.

Günter and I warmed up our thumbs. A Rolls Royce Corniche pulled over to the side of the road just after it whizzed past us. The driver was a beautiful woman about forty or so. *Très elègante.* We ran up to the car and I reached for the door handle. It was locked. I peered in the window. She was reading a map. I knocked on the window and motioned for her to unlock the door. She jumped! She screamed! She drove off like a bat out of hell! Apparently she had not stopped to pick us up. I guessed that she was probably driving to the nearest police station to charge me and/or us with attempted rape and/or kidnaping and/or something. Fortunately, a VW bus scooped us up before they could apprehend us.

We continued our flight in an antique Mercedes, followed by a Volvo, followed by a '58 Ford Flip-Top Fairlane and climaxing with a flatbed truck . . . us on the flatbed. Two drunk Arabs in the cab.

There were a billion brilliant stars in the Moroccan sky that night. No moon. Eighty degrees. Lying on gunny sacks. Surrounded by fifty-gallon oil drums. Hands down the front of my pants!

"Günter!"

"They cannot see us back here."

Whatever happened to that shy boy I was pursuing? Once he got started, there was no stopping him. Who wanted to?

At about four in the morning, we pulled into a truck stop. Did I say truck stop? Change that to a shed with two cots, one table, four chairs, one stove, twenty oil drums and a five-foot-three-inch prune. The innkeeper/cook/gas station attendant was leathery, crinkly, dry. Our chauffeurs took coffee from the stove and offered some to Günter and me. Did I say coffee? Change that to crank-case oil. Used. They all drank it. I gagged. Then the old gentleman cooked breakfast. Did I say breakfast? Change that to Eggs ala Mobil Oil. They all ate it. I gagged. The man got some bread out of a crate in the corner. Thank god, I thought, I finally get to eat something. He dipped the bread into the frying pan, swished it around and then offered it to us. They all. . . . you know.

I belched 10-40W for the next three hours. Günter fell asleep as soon as we got back on the road. I wrote in my journal:

> Why am I so afraid of him? So in awe of him? I seldom say what I mean. . .and never what I feel. It's like Grant all over again, only with sex. I thought sex would make all the difference. It doesn't. Now I don't know what to think, to do. Maybe as we get to know each other better it will get easier. I hope so. I miss the others, especially Stacey, but when two people are just beginning a relationship, they need to be alone more—to get acquainted (and to drive each other crazy!)

Fez was unbelievable! It was a walled city. No vehicles were allowed inside that wall. There were no streets big enough. Donkey and pony carts carried goods from the huge docking area at the edge of the city to the interior reaches of that ancient fort.

The people all wore burnouses . . . or the equivalent. The only way you could tell a person's wealth was by the amount of gold in his(er) teeth. Mostly his. There weren't very many hers running around in public.

No tourists and thus no tourist accommodations . . . that I could see anyway. Everything was old. Everything was brown; nothing like the all-white, French-influenced cities near the coast. Narrow passages. Thick walls. Small rooms. Steep staircases. Low doorways. Indoor plumbing. Did I say plumbing? Change that to a cold water faucet in our old small brown room. And! Wait'll you hear this! Out in the hall, there is a closet. Inside that closet, there is a hole in the floor. Sitting next to that hole in the floor, there is a bucket of water. Inside that bucket of water, there is a brush. Right in front of that hole in the floor, there are two indented footprints facing the door. That's it! Good luck! Don't call me when you're through.

Günter and I had a wild dinner our first night in Fez. Unlike cosmopolitan Casablanca where the inhabitants speak a myriad of languages, Fez is rural and isolated and monolingual. And unfortunately that single language is sort of a French-ala-Arabique. Unintelligible to the Western ear. We had to cluck-cluck and oink-oink our dinner order. Günter and I were pretty embarrassed by it all, but our waiter had a terrific time. He was very talented. Great style! His interpretation of veal was extraordinarily moving, especially the part in Scene 2 where they take the poor little calf off to the slaughterhouse. I cried.

Günter told me that that was one of the reasons he liked me — because I was *simpático*. That is one of the nicest compliments one person can ever give another.

The stupid dictionary says that simpático means congenial or likeable. That's typically inadequate of the English language. There is no word in English that parallels simpático. Our waiter was simpático because he felt something for that baby cow and what he was feeling was not what we refer to as sympathy. He actually understood what that poor, cute little veal-to-be was experiencing.

I'll tell you what simpático means! Along about my junior year in high school, I developed some weird kind of acne on my back. The real nasty kind — as big as boils, dozens of them, filled with pus and usually bleeding. I still had the condition in college. I went for almost four years without taking my T-shirt off in front of another person. It made it very difficult to go to bed with anyone.

Grant asked me one night why I never took my shirt off. I tried to bluff my way out of it, but he was in a stubborn mood that night and just kept pushing me. I had become ashamed of my ugly mess. It wasn't just the embarrassment—I felt like a leper. Diseased! At first he was just teasing me, but when he saw how upset I was getting, he became gentle and understanding. I was sitting at the kitchen counter on a bar stool. He stood right behind me and put his hands on my shoulders.

"Don't please," I said.

"Tad, whatever it is, don't keep it inside," he said.

"Okay. I have a skin problem."

"Is that all?"

"It's really bad."

"Let me see."

"No."

"We all get pimples, man."

"Not like this, we don't."

He put his arms around me and pressed his chest against my back.

"I'll still love you even if you get leprosy."

"Thanks."

"I didn't mean it that way. I just meant . . ."

"It's okay. I understand."

He released his hug and started to pull my shirt up in the back.

"Don't!"

"Shut up, asshole!"

He pulled the shirt all the way up to my shoulders, then forced it off over my head. He stood there silently for a moment, then put both hands flat out on the middle of my back.

"Don't touch it!"

"Why not?"

"Because it may be viral, transmittable."

"I don't care."

"I do."

He rubbed my back slowly, never putting pressure on any of the tender spots. I was falling apart. He stopped suddenly and came around to my side. He was holding his hands up in front of him like a just-scrubbed surgeon waiting to be gloved.

"Go wash your hands," I said.

"This is what I think of your goddamned leprosy!" he said and put his hands on his face.

My body shook.

He threw his arms around me and we both held on for dear life. I think we both started bawling.

Now that is what simpático means! Congenial my ass! Webster can go fuck himself!

My acne cleared up after that, by the way. I don't mean to imply that it was some healing miracle. Whatever chemical imbalance I had in my system was obviously aggravated by my emotional reactions. I stopped feeling like a leper and I stopped being one.

Hey Grant!

Thought about you last night and decided it was about time I wrote to you. You guys must think I've really gone off the deep end this time. I guess I have! And it feels pretty damn good. Today anyway.

My apologies and love to Jeanie (tell her I'll write to her soon) but for right now, this is just for you.

I want to try and put into words how I feel now about what happened with us. I may never completely understand it, but I have changed my thinking somewhat.

I was (am) going through some kind of an identity thing and some, or a great deal of it is sexual. I told you I loved you and I made it sound like it was mostly a love-making kind of love—because I thought it was. I thought if I loved you, I had to also want to make love to you. You don't know how guilty that made me feel.

Then, in my usual fucked-up way, I overreacted and overadjusted. I've met a guy over here that I think I love. (I hope this doesn't embarrass you too much—yes I do, it's good for you!) Anyway, with all that guilt I was feeling about you, I swung the pendulum so far that when

I met this guy, I thought that wanting to make love to him meant that I didn't really love him.

Now I'm not sure how any of this love stuff is supposed to work, but I'm trying to just relax and see if some of my confusion will go away. Sure would be nice for a change!

My guess is that you guys have already forgiven me for crawling into bed with you that night and for the chaos that followed. That's what friends do! And I think that I've finally figured out that is what we are!

And that's all I have to say.

> I love you.
> Your friend Tad

Günter and I had decided we'd been spending an inordinate amount of time in bed together and that we ought to take a breather . . . separately, so as not to get on each other's nerves.

The wildest thing I saw in my wandering was a camel auction. Right in the middle of the city. There must have been over a hundred of those ugly things standing out there spitting and pissing. There was so much dromedary urine that they had rigged up a trough system running through the pens and then off to this sluice sort of thing where they siphoned the stuff into barrels to cart it out of the city . . . probably to be used as fertilizer on nearby farms.

I wanted to buy this one really cute camel that reminded me of the one in the Raggedy Ann and Andy story. It looked so depressed. But I suppose I'd be depressed too if I looked like that—Ubangi-lipped, droop-necked, hunch-backed, pig-tailed and baggy-kneed. That camel wasn't just sad; that camel was singin' the blues!

Günter said that I should've bought it so we could ride it across the desert to Egypt. With my luck, he'd be the one riding and I'd wind up walking the lead with the fucking camel eating my hair!

"We could both do it," Günter said, trying to talk us out of our virginities. Yeah, him too. At least he said he was.

"Not at the same time, we can't," I said.

"Do you want to go first?"

"First which way?" I asked.

"Either way."

God this is difficult, I thought. Then and now.

I giggled. I don't know why. I should've screamed. It hurt!

I think I giggled because he said, "*Ich liebe dich*," and what I thought was, "I *liebe* your dick, too!" I felt bad about giggling because he'd said it in German, which meant a lot more than if he'd said it in English. One's second language doesn't hold the same deep emotions as one's native tongue.

I also giggled because I wondered if he thought it was necessary to say "I love you," because of what we were doing.

I also giggled because I suddenly understood what that first time must mean to women.

I decided that the whole world of heterosexual activity . . . and maybe homosexual too . . . would be vastly improved if males had to be deflowered before being allowed to deflower any females. The experience would make men far more understanding and appreciative and caring. If a man didn't want to have it done by another man, his would-be mate could use her vibrator or whatever on him.

What a scene that would be: "You wanna fuck do you, lover boy? First, *you* gotta roll over!" That'd change a few tunes, wouldn't it?

"*Ich komme!*" Günter screamed!

"Me too!"

Apparently I was going to have to wait awhile for my turn on top. We smoked. Post-coital cigarettes. Tradition.

I thought about that dumb pantyhose commercial about feeling good all under. I blushed.

"What is wrong?" Günter asked.

"Absolutely nothing," that I could think of.

"You got red."

"Just warm."

"*Gut*. Me too."

"I have to talk to you about something," I said as my passive attitude began to fade. Sometimes I don't know when to keep my mouth shut.

"What?"

"I was thinking . . . if you came back to the States with me . . ."

"And do what?"

"I don't know. Work, I guess. Then in a couple of years, we . . ."

"Tad!"

"What?"

"Please do not plan so far in advance."

"But if we're going to live together, we have to . . ."

"We do not know what is going to happen. We are together now. That is all we know."

"But we have to . . . you can't . . ."

"Stop trying to make everything fit the way you fantasize it to be!"

"I'm not!"

"Then why are you bringing all this up now?"

"I saw you in that bar today."

"Yes?"

"You were hustling that guy."

"Just for money."

"I wish you wouldn't do that anymore."

"Why?" he asked.

"Because I . . . because we mean something to each other now and I . . ."

"We need the money," he said.

"No we don't."

"You have found a way to live without money?"

"No, I have some money." One of these days, I'm going to have that mouth sewn up.

He just stared at me.

"I've had it all along. I was saving it in case I got into trouble. We're in trouble now."

"Yes, we are." There was a strange tone to his voice.

"I don't think you mean the same thing."

"You do not learn. You . . ."

"I . . ."

"You do not learn!" he shouted. "You still think you have to pay for me! I do not want you to pay for me! William did not throw me out like I told you! I left there because I wanted to be with you! You do not understand what love is! You do not understand me! I cannot be with you this way!!"

I couldn't speak. I was stunned. You would've thought I'd called his mother a *Scheisskopf* or worse the way he carried on. And the way he packed his bags. And the way he walked out the door. And the way he didn't come back.

I grabbed the travelers cheques out of my bag and glared at them. I was going to rip them to shreds! It was all their fault! I didn't. I couldn't. I didn't have enough (cou)rage!

"I can't even get upset properly!" I screamed aloud. "And I didn't get my goddamn turn!!"

17. El Autobús She Got Bang Bang!

Have you ever been so frustrated and so angry (are they the same?) that you wanted to kill someone? I have. There is a heavy and wonderful scene in the movie *Day of the Locust*, (or was it *Locusts*?) in which Donald Sutherland stomps to death this sexless kid in a parking lot. I knew how he felt. I almost killed a little kid once.

That baby I saw over at Charley's house the day they moved in next door unfortunately grew up. It turned out to be a boy. He was a little shit.

Charley's dad's name was Chester. The mom was Charlene. I guess Charley was named after her. I wondered if that made him a junior. The brat was a junior, but they called him little Chet. It should've been coitus interruptus. That little prick broke up more boy sex than Anita Bryant could hope to in her lifetime. I swear that kid could smell an erection four rooms away. Every time Charley and I would get going good, Chet would come busting into the room.

I remember one day Charley and I were going at a little mutual masturbation (M&M's we kids used to say and then giggle) when darling little Chet came waltzing into Charley's bedroom and asked what we were doing. I told him that we were playing with each other's peepee and that if he didn't get the hell out of there in the next two seconds, I was gonna bite his off!

Of course, he ran screaming to his mommy. Charley told her that he and I were playing with his *beebee* gun and I had told Chet he was too young. She didn't believe it, but she didn't do anything about it either. She didn't even call the Mother to tell her. I don't think she liked the Mother any more than I did.

So, anyway, Chester, Charlene, Charley, Chet and I all went up to the lake one Sunday afternoon. Right after the picnic lunch, Charley and I took off for the secluded spot where we always went for skinny-dipping and messing around. Strangely enough, we were able to get through the swimming and the messing around before Chet interrupted us.

I was already back into my swim trunks, but Charley was still naked and in the middle of a piss, when the screaming started. That meant I had to be the one to go see what was wrong with the little brat.

I froze in my tracks. Chet was standing in the middle of a small clearing just screaming away as loud as he could. No wonder! There was a large rattlesnake about three feet from his left foot. Coiled and rattling!

I found a big, heavy stick — practically a log — and walked slowly over to them. What a scene! The kid was screaming! The snake was screaming! I was screaming!

I knew I had to beat one of them to death! After some thought, I decided I'd better do the snake. That little fucker Chet wasn't even grateful to me for saving his life. All he did was ask me what Charley and I had been doing out there by ourselves.

Anyhow, that's how I felt when Günter walked out of my life. I wanted to kill him. Then I turned that anger inside . . . and wanted to kill me. Either way, it's scary!

He bolted the door, closed the windows and the blinds, then sat down at the small writing table next to the bed. There was a so-ugly-it-was-cute ashtray holder on the table that was supposed to be a camel lying down like a cat (something a camel cannot do) so that its legs came out around the sides of the shallow well in which an ashtray would sit if someone hadn't stolen it. It looked like it was hand-carved and hand-painted. In the States, the holder would've been stolen along with the ashtray. In Fez, no one wants to look at camels any more than (s)he has to.

He took his just-purchased pistol out of the drawer and placed it between the camel's legs. He found a piece of paper in the drawer and wrote:

Günter,

I tried to love you. I'm sorry.

Tad

He tore the slip of paper into tiny pieces and threw them into the small wastebasket (a ceramic urn actually) under the table. He took out another piece of paper and wrote:

Trish,

Things just never seem to work out the way I plan. The nicest thing that ever happened to me in my life was meeting you.

I love you.

Tadpole

He folded the paper in half, wrote her name on it and propped it up behind the camel. He rested his fingers on the camel's baggy knees, staring into its eyes. He thought for a moment that he saw a tear in the camel's eye. "When the camel cries, the battle is lost," the legend says.

The camel gave him the gun.

He sat for several very long minutes, just rubbing the gun with his fingers and watching the camel to see if it was going to cry again. It didn't.

He put the gun to his temple.

He sang "The Baggy-Kneed Camel Blues!"

He pulled the trigger.

CLICK!!!!

There aren't enough exclamation points in the world to illustrate the loudness or impact of that Click! Your whole life is compacted into that Click! Everything you've ever done is in that Click! Everyone you're ever loved is in that Click! I think that's what I like best about The Suicide Game—it has drama!

It always reminds me just how much I really do want to live!

The cap pistol you use should look as much like the real thing as possible. That's important. I've used those phony pistol cigarette lighters, but they require a lot more imagination and concentration. You have to convince yourself that the gun is real, otherwise it won't scare the shit out of you when you pull the trigger. But be careful. There's evidence that some people can convince themselves so totally that something is real that it actually becomes real to them, with real consequences! You wouldn't want to scare yourself to real death! Oh! Be sure to double-check, every time, that it is a toy pistol you are using.

The suicide note is not essential, but I think it helps to focus your thoughts and unload your mind. It should be to the person you feel the strongest about at the moment, so it can be either someone you feel a lot of love for or the person you hate the most, other than yourself. I think it's more helpful to express love and not try to blame somebody else for your fucked-up circumstances.

When I play the game now, it's either just for fun or as a little reminder because the first time I played it, and actually believed it, it convinced me beyond a shadow of a doubt that I could never kill myself. Misery is one thing. Death is another.

And I was miserable. But I had a plan.

Well Trish,

I've really blown it this time (and that is not a pun). I'm afraid I've chased Günter away for good. And I'm lost. My first impulse was to go running to you. But I think this might be the time for me to try out that dream I had about burnouses and sand and camels. The image I had of becoming a nomad and a seer has gotten pretty blurry lately, but it is still there and I'm just in the mood to play with it.

I feel pretty good about everything today. Even a little bit excited. Adventure awaits me! I might even meet some new people, huh? That oughta make you happy.

I thought I'd sell or give away the stuff I have left (got rid of most of it on the way to see you in Casa—those damned bicycles!) and get myself a nice warm burnous and whatever that lighter-weight thing they wear underneath is called. I've been wandering around out in the sun this week, so I'm already darker. And I don't have any gold on my front teeth, so I shouldn't get robbed—they'll all think I'm poor. I am. But not broke—so don't worry.

I'll keep writing to you (I won't have an address for a while) at the *pensión*, so if you leave there, give them your forwarding address.

I still expect to see you in Vancouver one of these days or years. I have not gone out of your life forever!

Love ya,

Tadpole

P.S. Thought you might enjoy the enclosed poem. It's the way I felt yesterday. I feel better (different) today.

O DREAMS!

I stand waivering on the
very brink of reality . . .
frightened by my expectations . . .
knowing well that
life won't compete with my dreams.

I am forever taunted by the
mirages of my mind . . .
disappointed at each step
by fantasized plots gone awry . . .
left always with an empty heart.

O Dreams! Sweet Beautiful Dreams!
I languish in your delicate fabric.
I thrive in your delusions.
I suffer in your whimsy.
I die in your promise.

—Tad Prescott

I kissed the camel on the nose and went out to mail the letter and poem to Stacey.

When I got back to the room, I bolted the door and closed the windows and the blinds. I took off my clothes. I shaved for the first time in three days. I soaked a towel in the cold water and sponged myself off. I rubbed lotion all over my body—my poor dry skin soaked it up in seconds. I pulled the bedspread and blanket off the bed and stretched out on my back on the cool sheet. And, for the first time in a lot of years, I was able to turn myself on without fantasizing. I felt good!

Hi Mom,

Just woke up from a little nap and thought I'd let you know I'm all right. Did you see that postmark? Bet you thought no son of yours would ever be writing to you from Fez! It is one wonderful place! You can feel the history here. Centuries of it.

For the moment, I'm traveling alone, but it's nothing to be concerned about. I'm safe—it's nothing like L.A. I'll probably be rejoining the friends I met in Barcelona before too long anyway. Right now, I'm going to see a little more of North Africa. As a matter of fact, I have to catch a bus right now . . . so I'll have to say good-bye.

I'm sorry I sent you that odd poem, "Afrika!" I guess I was just trying to rile you. I am sorry.

Your loving son,

Tad

Amazing how new insights come with the loss of one's virginity. I was standing in line at the bus ticket window when I thought of a female equivalent for the pain of having your balls smashed with a sledge hammer. The line could be something like: or would you rather give birth to a thirty-pound porcupine? Yeah, that'd hurt.

I got up to the window.

"How much is a ticket to Cairo?" I asked.

The clerk mumbled something in French-ala-Arabique.

"Je ne parle pas français. ¿Habla usted español?"

"No."

"*El hombre dice que los revolucionarios en el desierto están tirando a los autobuses*," a European-looking woman in purple standing behind me in line said.

I had to think that one out. *El hombre dice.* The man says. *Los revolucionarios.* The revolutionaries. *En el desierto.* Easy, in the desert. *Están tirando.* Don't know that one. *A los autobuses.* At the buses. Okay—the revolutionaries in the desert are something at the buses. *Tirando. Tirando.* Target? No, shooting! That's it! The revolutionaries in the desert are shooting at the buses!

"The revolutionaries in the desert are shooting at the buses?!!!" I screamed at her!

"*Sí, sí, señor*! *El autobús* she got bang bang!" the purple woman said, jumping up and down excitedly.

"Oh, you speak English, too?" I asked her.

"Yes. Very well, thank you," she said accentedly.

"I don't mean to be rude, but 'El autobús she got bang bang' is not well English," I said rudely.

"I know, but I heard it in an American movie years ago and I've been dying to use it ever since," she got me.

"Will you excuse me, please?" I said politely.

"Certainly," she said.

"One-way to Barcelona, please," I said to the ticket clerk.

Good grief.

"Pst."

There goes my career as a seer.

"Psst."

I don't have the right build for a burnous anyway.

"Pssst!"

It will be great to see Stacey again.

"PSSSST!!"

"What is it?!"

The man was cloaked. Hood down over the face. The whole bit. I expected him to whip out a plucked chicken any time. He motioned me off to the side. I was cautious. I left myself plenty of running room.

"Howya doin' kid?"

"Fine, and you?"

He pulled the hood back off his face.

"Wally!!" I shouted.

"Shhhh!!" he shushed me.

"What the hell are you doing here?" I asked.

"Trying to stay out of prison," he said.

"Makes sense," I said.

"Are the others with you?"

"They went back to Barcelona. The company said they'd take care of them from there."

"That's good. Nice bunch of kids."

"Is Hermes with you?"

"No, he said he was going to try and make it back to the States," Wally said.

"What are you going to do?"

"Just stay here. I've got a fresh chicken stand in the central market. There are so many people running around there and so much noise all the time that no one has figured out yet that I don't speak a word of their language."

"That I can relate to."

"What are you doing?"

"Just on my way back to Barcelona, too."

"Good idea. It's safer there."

"Did you hear they're shooting at the buses coming across the desert?"

"Happens all the time."

A large, horse-drawn cart came speeding down the narrow street. Without a driver! Right at us!

"What the hell is . . . ?" Wally yelled.

"Wally!! Look out for the . . . !!!" I screamed.

Holy shit! The cart hit a big rut in the road and the barrels in the cart broke loose and went flying all over the place.

Two of them landed on Wally.

They were the same barrels I'd seen at the camel auction. They were full. The stench was appropriate.

"Wally?" I cried. He was bleeding at the mouth.

"Piss?" he asked.

"Piss," I answered.

"Shit!" he said.

"Yeah," I said.

People were starting to gather near us. Wally pulled an oilskin pouch out of his robe and handed it to me.

"Take this," he said.

"But . ."

"Take it. If the piss doesn't get me, the cops will. Just take it and go!"

"But I . . ."

"Now! Get out of here!"

I did. I ran to the bus. I looked back just in time to see half-a-dozen uniformed men pull Wally's limp body out from under the barrels and drag it away.

I sat in the back of the bus. I untied and opened Wally's oilskin pouch. There were a bunch of papers from the *Reporte Internationale*, a map of North Africa and about THIRTY THOUSAND DOLLARS IN CASH!!

18. The Mist of Your Dream

"We can't keep that money!" Stacey argued.

(The trip from Fez to Barcelona was long, lonely and laborious. My reunion with Stacey & Co. at *El Pensión de las Flores* was gabby, giggly and gushy.)

"The hell we can't!" shouted Biff.

"It's drug money," Mike said.

"We don't know that," Toby said and got a scolding glare from Mike.

"Where is the money?" Biff asked.

"It's safe," I assured him.

"We need it to get back to Vancouver, don't we?" asked Dierdre.

"No, we don't," Stacey said. "The company already said they were paying our way back to Canada, plus our salaries, commissions and severance. Which reminds me, Tad doesn't know about our dinner date."

"What dinner date?" I asked.

"We have all been invited to dinner this Saturday night at the home of none-other-than W.H. Richardson himself!" she announced proudly.

"Who's he?" I wondered.

"Only the publisher of *Reporte Internationale* and countless other magazines."

"Big time," I observed.

"You haven't heard the kicker," Toby nudged me.

"What?"

"The invitation included one Tad Prescott, Esquire."

"You're kidding?"

"Nope, you're invited."

"Why would he invite you? How would he even know about me?"

"We don't know," Mike said. "The secretary just told us to bring you."

"But you didn't know I'd be here."

"She seemed to know."

"Very weird."

"Can we get back to the money now?" Biff asked.

"Yeah," Toby said and got another glare from Mike. "Will you please stop glaring at me like that."

"I will when you stop worrying about that damned money!" Mike told him.

"You're just thinking of yourself. The company'll take care of us, but what about Tad? He's stuck here!" Toby argued generously.

"Oh yeah, I know that's your biggest concern."

"Well, it is a concern."

"Will you please stop!" I said. "I have a little money in reserve and I'm expecting my mother to send my last paycheck any time now."

"She did," Stacey said, fumbling in her purse. "Here. It came a couple of days ago."

"Well, that's settled then," I said and stuck the envelope in my pocket.

"Aren't you going to open it?" Stacey asked.

"Later."

"I just thought of something," Mike said. "What if Wally shows up asking for his money back?"

"Wally's dead," Biff said.

"I didn't say he was dead," I told him. "I said he was limp."

"So, he's either dead or in prison. He ain't gonna be asking for the money!" Biff insisted.

"Which brings us back to whether or not it is drug money," Stacey said.

"We don't know," Dierdre added.

"What else could it be?" I asked. "We're fairly certain he was dealing and he couldn't have made that much money selling magazines."

"So what if it is?" Biff said. "Who do we return it to? The Mob?"

"He has a point there," Dierdre waivered again.

"We return it to the police," Mike said.

"We could do that," I said. "We'd probably get it back if no one claimed it. Legally and rationally, that seems to be the thing to do. But emotionally, I'm not convinced. I can't stop thinking about what that money represents. I keep getting images of these sleazy pushers hanging around junior high schools handing out free samples to kids to get them started, then bleeding them dry after they get them hooked on one thing or another. I saw this student film once, made by a high-school kid, which had this boy about fifteen who was a real pill freak and, at the beginning of the film, he puts on a record—it was one of Streisand's offbeat albums—and sits on his bed taking one pill after another and tripping to the music. The idea was that once he got into it, he didn't even realize he was still eating the pills, one after another. The music gets really, uh, moanful, wailing, and the kid starts going under, but when he falls back on the bed he begins to puke. By then, he can't even move, so the vomit just flows up out of his mouth and runs down the sides of his face and over his chin onto his neck. He chokes a couple of times and then dies. I can't even think the word drug without remembering that boy's face."

"Jesus!" said Mike.

"I think we should give the money to charity," I concluded.

"So do I," Mike voted.

"Agreed," Toby said, then dug into his bag and pulled out a small envelope of what sounded like pills. He threw it in the wastebasket.

"Charity," Stacey said and looked at Dierdre.

"Okay," Dierdre said.

We all looked at Biff. He was sitting there just staring. At me. I don't think he and I had ever made eye contact before, but at that moment he was making up for it. He was looking inside my head and seemed to be wanting me to look inside him. I could feel him thinking: What is happening here? It was eerie. He was pulling me. I had to break the contact. I looked at his nose.

"Okay, charity," Biff said.

There was a strange electricity in the room, then a snap and people were moving around again. Stacey was at my side.

"Come to Vancouver with us," she said.

"I might," I told her. "I need to think."

I went to my room. I plopped down on the bed and opened the envelope. I noticed that the Mother didn't tear off the little narrow border that is always on stamps that were on the outside edges of a sheet of stamps. In her prime, she never failed to neatly tear off that little border. The old girl was mellowing . . . finally. There was a money order, a letter from Grant and a letter from the Mother.

Dear Son,

I hope this money order gets to you all right. I hate sending it like this, not knowing for certain that you will get it. Everyone at the bank has been very understanding. Ruth, especially. She says she thinks you can get your old job back if you want it when you get over this problem you are having. Did you know that her husband is a psychiatrist? He's a very interesting man. They've had me over for bridge several times since you left. Ruth's mother is our fourth. That poor old woman is eighty-five now and is getting so senile. Half the time she can't remember the bids or the trump suit. But Lord knows she'll be passing on soon, so I don't really mind putting up with her forgetfulness. She deserves all the pleasure she can get out of her last years.

On the nights when 'granny' (that's what everyone calls her) is too sick to play, Ruth's son sits in for her. Have you met Raymond? He's about your age. He's going for his doctorate in some branch of sociology at UCLA. He's a wonderful boy. And an excellent bridge player as well.

I enjoyed your little poem about Africa. But you know how I am. I'm the more traditional type—I like my poetry to rhyme. You may send me more of your poems if you like. You seem to enjoy writing them. I did not, however, appreciate your phonetic spelling of M. Rimbaud's name. I am not illiterate.

Grant asked me to enclose the note from him. He and Jeanie seem to care for you very much. You should take advantage of that friendship. I guess young people sometimes feel they have to travel the world, but you should remember that when you get older, it's home and friends that matter the most.

Grant is such a nice young man, but he should clean up his language. You tell him I said so.

Well, I have to run. Bridge tonight. Let's hope that 'granny' can tell the hearts from the spades.

Please take care of yourself. And write again.

Mother.

You Fucking Asshole!!

If I ever catch you sneaking out of our house (and 'our' means me, Jeanie and you!) in the middle of the night, I'm going to beat the shit out of you. Is that clear?

You think we're going to stop loving you because of one little misunderstanding? Or even a dozen? Yeah, we were both upset when you got into bed with us (you are a very strange person, Tad) but you didn't hang around long enough for us to straighten it out. You know that Jeanie and I fight sometimes. And we always make up. Well, we can fight . . . have arguments with you and make up too! Like you said, that's what friends do!

So, get your ass back here! Or, if you're having a really good time, write to us and then come back when you're ready. We're here when you need us.

I don't know anything about this love (sex) stuff with other guys, so I'm not a good one to ask for advice. If you do love that guy you wrote about, and he loves you, then I don't see what could be wrong with it. I'm all for anything that'll make you happy. I know you could use some of that now.

Okay friend? I hope you are okay. Come back and live with us if you want to. Or just come for a visit. Or write. Do anything— just know that we care!

You stupid shit!

Love,

Grant

P.S. Jeanie says Hi! And Love! And ditto to above!

I went for a very long walk. And a talk. With myself.
What the hell am I supposed to do now? I asked me. Go to Vancou-

ver with Stacey? Go back to L.A. and live with Grant and Jeanie again? Search the world for Günter?

I went up the big hill that Günter and I had walked up when we first met. The sun was either just coming up or just going down.

Vancouver. I'd be with Stacey. And with MikenToby. Lots of gay bars there. And baths. Shouldn't be too hard to find a job. B and D would be there, but we probably wouldn't spend much time with them anyway. MikenToby could introduce me to some of their gay friends. But I wonder if I would have to get a work permit? Me with a green card?! That's a strange thing. Always thought of others as the foreigners, the aliens. Probably need a visa just to live there.

I wandered around the downtown area. There were maybe millions of people dashing about. It must've been lunchtime.

Maybe I should go back to Los Angeles, I thought. I should have given Grant and Jeanie a chance to work things out with me, since they know how to do that sort of thing. I get so carried away. Overreact. They were fun to live with. But what if I got weird about Grant again? Or crawled into bed with them again? And the bank! Could I go back to work there? No. And the Mother!?!

I walked through the harbor district, past my old hangouts, but I didn't feel like going into any of the bars.

Maybe I should go looking for Günter. He probably came back to Barcelona. He's probably shacking up with William again. Or maybe with Pamela, if she came back from Amsterdam.

Fuck, I don't know what to do.

I wound up at the *Santa María* once, but I was afraid to go aboard. That cop might be around . . . the one who threw us off the ship that morning, cursing our blasphemous behavior. Besides, I didn't really need to see that bunk Günter and I shared that night.

Eenie, meenie, minie moe . . .
To Vancouver should I go?
Is it back to good ol' L.A.?
Or is Barcelona the only way?

I couldn't find a three-sided coin to toss.

As a kid, whenever I couldn't make up my mind about something, the Mother always said that I should trust in the Lord. And I always told her that feudalism was dead. And she always hit me.

I watched a flower vendor closing her stall. All of her flowers were white . . . except one, which was red-red. She gave it to me, saying it would bring me luck. I guess I lost it somewhere.

I liked Charley's way of deciding stuff. If he had to make a decision, he'd just stand on his head. That's all! He just stood on his head! Until he totally forgot whatever it was that he was supposed to decide about. Problem solved! I was never very good at standing on my head. Charley could do it anywhere, anytime. I always fell over.

I tried it when I finally got back to the room. It seemed like I'd been gone an awfully long time—the room didn't even look familiar to me. I took a pillow from the bed and put it right in front of the door. I got down on my knees and placed my hands just so. Charley said you're supposed to make a triangle with your head and hands. I did. I kicked up. Smashed into the door. My cigarettes and lighter fell out of my shirt pocket and hit me on the chin. I braced my arms and slowly eased my legs away from the door. I did it! I was standing on my head! Unaided!

My vision started to blur. My head got tilted to one side somehow and I couldn't straighten it out. It was hurting the hell out of my neck. The worst part was that not only was I unable to forget my dilemma—I added a fourth alternative!

It occurred to me that I could just continue bumming around Europe. That's what I came here for in the first place. No reason I have to go back now. No reason Günter has to be in my life. I can see Stacey later.

A fifth alternative! I could run off with the money!

I fell down on that one! My right knee clobbered my nose as I doubled up. I wound up fetally in the middle of the floor. I did not get up.

Knock. Knock.

Who could that be? I know what I'll do! Whoever is on the other side of that door will determine my fate! Let's see. If it's Stacey, I'll go to Vancouver. If it's Mike, I'll look for Günter. If it's Toby, I'll go back to Los Angeles. If it's Biff, I'll run off with the money. Who else is around? Dierdre. If it's Dierdre, I'll . . . I'll commit suicide!

Knock. Knock.

I opened the door.

It was Señor Junior, floor scrubber extraordinaire!

I slammed the door!

Poor kid, probably all he wanted was a little blow job. Who knows? Maybe he actually came just to clean the room. It needs it. Oh well.

Knock. Knock.

"*Ocupado!*"

"Open the door, you weirdo!" MikenToby said.

I did.

"Where have you been?" they asked.

"Out walking."

"You've been gone for almost two days."

"Whataya mean I've been gone for almost two days?"

"I mean that you have been gone for almost two days."

"Where did I go?"

"We don't know."

"Well, where did I sleep?"

"We don't know."

"My god! I could've been killed out there."

"There's no need to get melodramatic."

"Death is melodramatic!"

"Were you with Günter?" one of them asked me.

"I don't even know where Günter is."

"Didn't he say in his note?"

"What note?"

"He left you a note a couple of days ago."

"Didn't Stacey give it to you?"

"STACEY!!!!"

I ran to her room. Barged in without knocking.

"Goddamn you!" I screamed.

"Tad! Where have you been?" she asked.

"Don't start that shit!"

"We've been so worried about you."

"You call it worried! I call it meddling! I call it . . . I call it interfering!"

"What are you talking about?"

"The note, goddamnit! The note from Günter!"

"Oh."

"OH!"

"Tad, I . . ."

"Don't Tadeye me! How dare you! I know I don't always make the so-called right decisions, but I do insist on making my own!"

"I wasn't trying to make decisions for you . . . I just didn't want you to get hurt anymore."

"But you have hurt me. More than he ever could. I trusted you!"

"I'm sorry," she said.

"Can I have my note, please?" I asked rudely.

"Yeah." She took it out of her purse and handed it to me. I stuffed it in my pocket.

"Thanks."

"Tad . . ."

I slammed the door and stomped off in the direction of my room. I tensed, knowing she was going to come charging out of her room any second and tackle me or something before I could get safely back to my room.

She didn't.

I walked back to her door and stood there for a moment thinking what I would say to her if I should decide to ever speak to her again. I raised my hand to knock, but my nerve failed me in the two inches between knuckle and door. I went back to my room, wondering why she hadn't come after me.

MikenToby were on my bed . . . massaging!

"Goddamnit!" I said.

"A little lower," one of them said.

"She takes it upon herself to decide what I should do and . . ."

"Now a little left."

". . . and then won't even go out of her way to make it up to me!"

"God, that's great!"

"What the hell are you doing?!" I demanded, but threw their asses out the door before they had a chance to answer. I braced the desk chair under the door knob. I unfolded the note.

Tuesday

Tad,

I saw you at the train station yesterday and yelled at you, but I guess you did not hear me. Then I lost you in the crowd. If you want to talk, please meet me at The Hill tomorrow morning at ten. I want to see you.

Ich liebe dich,
Günter

What's today? Thursday! I think. Shit! I wonder what day it was that I went up on the hill. I cannot handle this!

God! Talk about depression! I couldn't get out of bed! For two days! I think. I couldn't cry! I couldn't even fantasize! I was a sick boy! At one point, I found myself lying in bed, fully clothed with the covers pulled up under my chin. I was shaking. It was at least ninety degrees in the room.

I kept falling asleep and having quick snatches of dreams—dreams that scared me, but I couldn't make them come to mind when I woke up.

MikenToby banged on the door a couple of times, but I didn't let them in. Even Dierdre called through the door once. They wanted to console me. I guess Stacey didn't. Want to console me. Or I didn't hear her if she tried. Even though I was inconsolable, I might have let her try.

I thought I heard her voice once, but it must've been in a dream because when I opened the door, she wasn't there. It was particularly sweaty dream—my clothes were drenched. I relocked the door and went back to sleep.

Then I was naked, sitting on my pillow at the head of the bed. Hermes was sitting cross-legged at the foot of the bed. He was naked too, but his whole body was covered with hair, so it didn't matter if he had clothes on or not.

"The ant," Hermes was explaining, "as he climbs up the sides of the doodlebug cone only to fall back again, does not comprehend the fact that he is about to die. He is not struggling valiantly to save his own life, as you would have him doing. He is simply acting on instinct to get out of the hole into which he has fallen."

Hermes began to shed his hair all over the bed.

"Expectation is realistic; fantasies are merely hope," he said.

His hair was falling off in clumps and piling up on the floor next to the bed.

"As the poet said:

> I am forever taunted by the
>   mirages of my mind . . .
>   disappointed at each step
> by fantazied plots gone awry . . .
> left always with an empty heart."

Then he really was naked—all his hair was gone!

Then he was gone too.

Then I woke up. I got out of bed to get dressed only to discover that I was dressed. So I undressed, then put on my bicycling shorts. The ones that looked to me like they were mountain climbing shorts. The ones that Günter made for me the day we left *La Linea*. The ones that reminded me that he was gone. I put on my red sweater. The one that was supposed to add a dash of color to my drab wardrobe. The one that Günter bought for me the day we left Barcelona. The one that reminded me that he was gone.

Why does this happen to me? I thought . . . why do people disappoint me? . . they make me believe I can trust them, love them, then they fuck with my head . . . Stacey probably didn't really love me to begin with . . . I'm sure Günter never did . . . shit, even when people do love you, they forget to remind you that they do . . . I don't always remember myself . . . just a hug now and then . . . maybe a kiss . . . but a real one, not one of those social pecks that would better be left to a handshake . . . hugs are best . . . I need a hug now.

Depression—wallowing in self-pity, the complete absence of hope— may well be a dangerous pastime, but it does have some redeeming qualities. It provides a fair measure of catharsis, especially the kind of depression where you scream out a lot of painful stuff like "Why can't I love anyone?!" and "Where the hell are you god?!" and "Fuck me!!" Depression can also lead to its own type of convoluted clarity—a new insight or way of looking at yourself and life—if used sparingly and if you allow it to consume you entirely. You have to keep it going long enough to get a little information about yourself (sometimes it falters too early and you have to give it a boost), but you also have to learn when to come out of it!

Knock. Knock.

"Who's there?"

"Biff."

"Biff who?"

"Tad, I need to talk to you," he said.

I opened the door because I couldn't imagine what Biff could possibly have to say to me. The others I understood. Him, I did not.

"Thank you," he said as he entered and closed the door behind him.

I went back to bed.

He pulled the chair up next to the bed and straddled it backwards, thinking he looked more macho that way. He did.

"You look like shit," he said.

"I know."

"Are you all right?"

"No."

"Can I help?"

"Is your name really Biff?"

"As far as I'm concerned it is."

"Good for you."

He was looking at me that way again—soul to soul. Pulling.

"Are you all right?" I asked him.

"I don't know."

"You reacted so strangely to that story I told the other day about the kid with the drugs."

"I didn't even hear the story . . . because you were staring at me."

"I was staring at you?"

"Yeah, the whole time you were talking."

"I wasn't aware of it." I wasn't.

"I was."

"You didn't hear the story?" I asked.

"No."

"But you agreed to give the money to charity."

"Did I?"

"Yes. I thought it was because of the story."

"I don't think so. It felt like you suddenly saw inside me. I didn't like it."

"I thought it was the other way around."

"What was it all about?" he asked.

"I don't know. Our spirits touched or something. It happens sometimes. I don't know what it means. Some form of communication I guess."

"I thought maybe you were getting the hots for me or something."

"I don't think so," I said. I hoped not.

But then I wondered. Was I? No, that feeling was not a sexual one. It was me doing it though. He was right about that. I began to remember what I had felt when our eyes met. It was reaching . . . reaching for understanding . . . reaching for male love. Love-love. But you'd never be able to grasp that one, Biff. I have a hard time with it myself. It's because you're strong, confident. It's because you're masculine. It's because you're not gay. It's because . . . I need a father. But if I told you that, you'd say it was impossible because we're the same age and I would never be able to explain it to you. Now, if this were a movie, I wouldn't be afraid to tell you all this and we would talk it all out and I'd come to grips with it all and go about my life with a whole new perspective, somehow improved by my self-realization and somehow content in my newly acquired, adjusted state. Hm. Too bad.

"It's a good thing," Biff said in response to my denial of having lusted for him. "I don't care what you guys do with each other as long as you stay away from me."

"Yeah, I know. Hey, you know what it probably was? It was probably just that we were on the same wavelength at that moment about the money or the drugs or something."

"Just don't do it again. Okay?"

I wasn't sure if he wanted to beat me up. Or cry. Or both. His voice was strange. Tight. Suddenly I no longer felt intimidated by him, which was a little odd in that, until that second, I hadn't realized that I had felt intimidated by him. And for a fleeting moment, I kind of wished that I hadn't ignored him all along. The thought passed quickly.

"I'll do my best not to do it again," I told him, "but I don't think it's one of those things one can control."

"If you say anything to them about this, I'll punch your lights out."

"I won't."

"C'mon," he said, pulling me off the bed. "I think you oughta go with us to that dinner."

"Is it Saturday already?"

"Uh huh."

"I lost some time again."

"Come on!" he said and slapped me on the butt. I guess he played football in school.

"I don't know if I should."

"I do. You're going."

He was right. That's why they sent Biff in to talk with me — because he had the muscle. To drag me out of my room. And into Stacey's. They were all there. Dressed for the dinner with the publisher. Good ol' W.H.!

"I don't have anything to wear!" I protested, trying not to look at Stacey.

"You do now," Mike said.

"Tad," Toby said, "we don't have the beach house and the typewriter to give you, but we do have these!"

He stepped aside and on the bed were: A White Suit. A Straw Hat. A Pair of Espadrilles! Stacey had remembered my dream for the future.

"Now get dressed! We're all going to dinner!"

They went down to wait for the chauffeur who was being sent to pick us up. I stopped Stacey at the door.

"Howya been?" I asked.

"Okay, I guess. You?"

"Not so good."

"Better now?"

"Yeah."

"Good."

Silence

"I . . ." together.

You first. No you. Go ahead. Please. All right.

"I'm sorry," together.

"Me too," together.

"I was worried about you, Tadpole. I am worried about you."

"Me too, Trish. Me too."

"It'll be better."

"You seduced me."

"I what?"

"You seduced me into being your friend, into loving you, trusting you. I think that obligates you not to betray that trust, that love. I think . . . oh hell! I think I need a hug!"

She gave me the biggest, the hardest and the longest hug ever hugged. She even licked up a couple of tears from my cheek. Nice lady.

"I had a dream about Hermes," I told her.

"Oh yeah? Was he good?"

"Not that kind of dream! He was naked though, sort of. He lost all his hair."

"Oh my."

"He told me to stop . . . to stop playing 'Lions and Christians' with doodlebugs."

"Really?" she said, not having the faintest notion what I was talking about.

"Fantasizing," I clarified.

"Why?"

"Why what?"

"Why did he tell you to stop?"

"It was a dream!"

"I know. Jesus. Watch my lips! Why do you think you had a dream in which Hermes told you to stop fantasizing?"

"Oh. Uh . . . because . . . uh . . ."

"Because of 'fantasized plots gone awry, left always with an empty heart?'"

"Where did you . . . ?"

"You sent it to me, dummy!"

"Oh yeah."

"Your fantasies chased him away, didn't they?"

"Who?"

"I'm gonna hit you! Günter!"

"I guess so."

"So . . . ?"

She waited for me to pick it up from there. I didn't.

"So you're going to . . . ?"

She waited again. In vain.

"So! You are going to stop what?!?"

Stubborn woman.

"Fantasizing?"

She did hit me.

"I can't," I said.

"You know that daydreaming is just another form of closing your mind. You bitched that school and work required you to close your mind to what you call the real world, the truth. What the hell do you think you're doing when you wander off in your head all the time?!"

"But I need to! For my writing!"

"Fine! Do it for your writing. Not for your life!"

"You . . . I . . ."

"Fantasizing and introspection are not the same thing, you know!"

"I know, but . . ."

"You want all your affairs to end the way it did with Günter?"

"No."

"Then . . . ?"

She was doing that fill-in-the-blanks thing again.

"Tad, I'm not going through that again!"

"I don't know if I can stop damnit!"

"You can!"

"I can't!!"

"A friend told me once that a person could accomplish anything by using a little discipline," she said, trying to make me eat my own words. I did.

"Touché, Trish," I said, taking her arm. "Boy, I was afraid we'd never be friends again after that fight we had. It has always been my experience that confrontation means separation . . . permanent separation."

"Not with me it doesn't."

"I should've known that."

"We'd better get downstairs," she said.

I seemed to be handing her a piece of paper.

"What's this?"

"I don't know."

She unfolded the paper. It was a poem.

"Now I remember . . . I wrote that for you."

THE MIST OF YOUR DREAM

There is a rare
    and marvelous sensation
       upon awakening,
where reality is still a blur
and the shadows work
    with your sleepy imagination
to recreate the scene
    of your last dream.
There is a warm glow to this place.
    The lights are soft.
       The colors are soft.
Your lover is at your side.
Everything is just as it should be.
And you try with your very soul
    not to wake up,
hoping to remain forever in
    the mist of your dream.

            —Tad Prescott

19. Honor Thy Mother. . . .
And Thy Father (if thou hast one)

"What was that?" I asked as we pulled up in front of the W.H. Richardson estate.

"I didn't see anything," Stacey said.

"What'd it look like?" Mike asked.

"I don't know," I said. I could've sworn that I saw a large clump of hair around by the side of the house, but it was out of the corner of my eye (as they say) and when I looked again, it was gone.

The chauffeur had picked us up promptly at 8:15 and there we were in front of this beautiful manor promptly at 8:30. This was a different Barcelona from the one we all knew and loved. They didn't have chauffeurs and butlers in the harbor district.

We were butled into the drawing room. It looked like a living room. A very nice living room. The house was magnificent! The house was elegant! The house was rich! The house was William's!!

"Good evening," William said as he entered the room.

Stacey and I looked at each other agog. Günter's Sugar Daddy is our publisher?

Introductions around. He was better looking than I had remembered him to be. And younger. Attractive actually.

"Please call me William," he said as he shook my hand.

I'm not even sure I can talk, I thought, much less call anybody William.

"Yessir," I said.

Then a very beautiful woman came into the room. She was statuesque. She had shimmering blond hair (in a $100+ hairstyle) and piercing blue eyes. I think I was staring at her.

"Everybody, this is my wife Pamela," William said.

Pamela? Not *the* Pamela? Please? Oh, he couldn't have been sleeping with a couple? Could he?

We did our Mouseketeer bit:

"Mike!"

"Toby!"

"Stacey!"

"Tad!"

"Dierdre!"

Deedee hit Biff!

"Biff!"

"How charming," Pamela said charmingly. "Please, everyone be seated."

We sat.

"Tad, I assure you that chair will hold you," Pamela said to me with a very pretty smile. I felt like a schoolboy at the beginning of a crush on the pretty new school marm.

"Yes ma'am," I said.

"Tad, sit!" Toby said.

Apparently I had gotten preoccupied and had forgotten to sit down. I sat.

I wondered if this was the same Pamela and if they took turns with Günter or if they all slept together. The thought made me shiver.

"Mr. Richardson," Stacey said, "how did you know about Tad and that he'd be in Barcelona?"

"I'm embarrassed to say," William said.

"Well, I'm not," Pamela said. "There is this wonderful psychic I've been seeing and . . ."

"Hermes Trismegistus!!" everyone shouted, practically knocking poor Pamela off her settee.

"Why yes!" she exclaimed.

"Is he in Barcelona?" Stacey asked hopefully.

"No dear, I'm afraid he isn't. He said he had to return to San Francisco on some unfinished business. The day before yesterday, I think it was. I will miss his guidance."

I wondered if Hermes was that clump of hair I'd seen as we drove up.

They probably all thought I was being unsociable because I wasn't participating in the dicussion, but I just couldn't get my thoughts organized enough to contribute anything.

I heard MikenToby asking William something about San Francisco and he said an enormous amount of numbers in a row, which were probably telephone numbers and/or addresses on streets that were also numbers. Or maye it was code. I didn't know.

And I could've sworn I heard Stacey say something to William about going to school in Amsterdam! And I know I heard Pamela invite Stacey to visit them in Amsterdam on weekends and school holidays! I wondered if Stacey was going to have an affair with thcm, too! Maybe the four of them would get it on! Don't even think that!

Dierdre was studying Biff. My guess was that she was wondering whether or not he was going to be able to provide her with a lifestyle comparable to the one we were temporarily being allowed to glimpse at that evening. As a matter of fact, Biff had already been promised a job with some development corporation at the end of the summer. I was positive he'd be a big success and provide Dierdre with exactly the style of living she deserved.

"Perhaps Mrs. Richardson could suggest a charity," Dierdre said, trying to be sociable.

"Why don't we just give her the money?" Mike said.

"What money is that?" Pamela asked charitably.

"Our former supervisor gave Tad . . ."

"Huh?" I asked. I still wasn't keeping up with the conversation. There was just too much to think about.

". . . gave Tad," Stacey continued, "a pouch with thirty thousand dollars in it."

Pamela's eyes lit up. Some people get turned on by charity.

"From his drug dealings, I suspect," William said.

"You know about that?"

"For some time, but we were never able to catch him with anything."

"Can we just give the money to you," Mike said to both William and Pamela, "and have you give it to charity? We don't want it."

"Some don't," Biff said.

"You agreed," Toby said.

"I know," Biff looked at me.

"I'll handle it through the police," William offered. "Then I'm sure Pamela will find the perfect cause for your donation."

"I know just the one," Pamela said. "There is a home for unwed teenage mothers and . . ."

"Perfect!"

"Oh, there you are young man. I thought maybe you had decided not to join us after all," William said, looking at the doorway.

We all turned to look too.

It was Günter!

This is disgusting, I thought. It's bad enough that they share him, but to flaunt it in public like this is . . . is outrageous!

"I believe you've all met our son, Günter," William said.

Son?

Stacey, I screamed inside my head, I need your help! Now! My knees are collapsing! I'm gonna fall down right here in front of all these people! And him!

I guess she had really good reception or intuition because she was at my side in a flash, taking a firm hold on my elbow.

Günter was grinning at me. I may have stuck my tongue out at him. I hope not.

"Did you know?" I whispered to Stacey.

"No," she whispered back.

Cocktails were served and they all went on chitchatting as though they didn't know I was losing my mind! I read the instructions for the drink mixer that was sitting on the bar. The instructions were in French. I found them very interesting.

Someone took me by the hand and led me out on the terrace.

It was Günter.

"I am sorry about Fez," he said.

"Me too."

He stuck a cigarette in my mouth and lit it for me. He lit one for himself.

"I waited for you on the hill," he said.

"I didn't get your note in time," I told him.

"Would you have come?"

"I'm not sure. Probably."

"*Gut.*"

"So. William and Pamela are your parents, huh?"

"Yes," he said grinning.

"Are they, uh, English?"

"Yes."

"And?"

"Oh. I was born in Amsterdam. If you will remember, my father's headquarters are there."

"I remember."

"I lived there most of my life."

"You lied to me."

"I did not."

"You said that William was jealous because you spent the night with me."

"I said he was angry with me for being out all night," Günter remembered correctly.

"But you did say something about fighting with Pamela over hustling."

"Yes."

"But if . . . oh . . . yeah. Wait a minute! You were arm in arm with William on that ship!"

"Sometimes we actually like each other. We had all just had a very tense holiday at the house on Majorca and mother had to go to Amsterdam for some important charity event, so father and I spent the last few days trying to patch up our last big fight."

"You deliberately let me think you were . . . you were . . . uh, you know . . . with them."

"Yes."

"Why?"

"Because I do not like everyone knowing my business."

"You mean because you don't trust anyone . . . don't trust me."

"Maybe. I do now. Do you?"

"You ought to be more careful . . ."

"Do you?"

"I'm not sure. I'm a little confused right now."

"They are going back to Amsterdam next week."

"That's nice."

"That means that they will not be using the house on Majorca this year."

"Guess not."

It was too confusing to look into his eyes, so I was watching his mouth. He was still grinning. It was a cute grin, but (or because) it was a little lopsided. Once in while, the big tooth on the left side (his right side) would catch some saliva on it and glisten as it reflected the terrace lights. It was just like one of those dumb romantic toothpaste commercials you see on television.

"We could," he said.

"Could what?"

"Have the house on Majorca."

"Oh."

"It is right on the beach."

"What is?"

"The house."

"Oh yes."

The stars were blinking on and off like those annoying Xmas tree lights.

"There is a typewriter there," he said.

"Sure, with your dad's business and everything."

"You could use it. If you wanted to."

"Thank you."

"I mean if you wanted to write any poems about spies or anything like that."

"Oh!"

"Well? Do you want to?"

"Uhhh. Yeah . . . I want."

"*Gut*! This is one time I do not mind if they pay for me!"

"How long will we be in . . . never mind."

He smiled.

"Come, it is time to eat."

He led me back into the house. Those people were still chitchatting away. Günter walked over to talk with his father. William? His father? Pamela? His mother? Their publisher? Beach house? Me? Majorca? My mind????

I knew people were talking in the room, but I couldn't make out what they were saying. Then I realized that I had been staring at a chair for the longest time without putting a story to it. I tried to open my mind to that chair's objective existence. It was sitting between the settee and the bookshelves. It was an antique chair and it was built so you could fold the back of it down to make a stepladder for getting books off the higher shelves. In its chair mode, it was a beautiful piece — you would never suspect it was concealing a ladder within its bosom. Not until you examined it closely. And . . .

Someone touched my arm.

"Huh?" I jumped.

"Time to eat," Stacey said.

"Where is everybody?" I asked. I didn't know.

"In the dining room," she told me.

"Oh."

"Pamela said . . ."

"It's Pamela already, is it?"

"I think she's terrific," Stacey said.

"She is nice. What did she say?"

"She said I should visit them in Amsterdam."

"I thought I heard something like that. You're going back to school?"

"Uh huh."

"In Amsterdam?"

"William says they have a very good education program."

"He does?"

"Yes, he does. He knows the head of the department and he's sure he can get me in."

"You wouldn't be thinking of getting to know William better would you?"

"They're both wonderful people."

"You know what I mean!" It wasn't just the fact that I thought she should break that habit; I got the feeling that Pamela would make a formidable opponent.

"Don't be ridiculous!" Stacey said.

I wondered if Stacey and I would somehow be related if she was seeing William at the same time I was with Günter.

"Pamela also said that Günter was going to ask you to go to Majorca with him."

"She told you that?"

"Yes she did."

"I had no idea there were so many open-minded mothers in this world."

"Are you going?"

"Uh . . . yeah! Yes. I am. Yes! I am going!! I am going to Majorca with Günter! Where is Günter?"

"Dining room."

"Oh yes."

"I think it's wonderful!" Stacey said.

"You do?"

"Yes I do."

"I love you."

"And I love you."

"Gesundheit!" she said.

"Where?"

"You."

First we hugged. Then we kissed. Then we hugged again.

Günter came from the dining room to find out what had happened to us. Stacey yanked him into our embrace.

First we all hugged. Then we all kissed. Then we all hugged again.

I could see the three of us atop Mount Everest, having just completed our climb. The freezing wind penetrates our parkas, chilling us to the bone. We have to huddle close together to get warm and . . .

One of them said, "We've lost Tad again."

One of them said, "Not for long."

One of them groped me.